The Night Heroes:

Free Fall

by

Dr. Bo Wagner

Word of His Mouth Publishers
Mooresboro, NC

All Scripture quotations are taken from the
King James Version of the Bible.

ISBN: 978-0-9856042-8-8
Printed in the United States of America
© 2013 Dr. Bo Wagner (Robert Arthur Wagner)

Word of His Mouth Publishers
PO Box 256
Mooresboro, NC 28114
704-477-5439
www.wordofhismouth.com

Chapter One

West Virginia was many miles behind us. Curved, hilly, impossibly-twisted mountain roads had given way to the much flatter land of good old North Carolina, home to my family and me. For those who do not know, "Me" is Kyle Warner. If you have read our first adventure, *The Cry from the Coal Mine,* then you know that I am a PK, a preacher's kid, and that I have two sisters, Carrie and Aly. And if you haven't read that story, you know now anyway, since I just told you! My dad is an evangelist, which means that he travels from church to church preaching meetings, and all of our family comes along with him. Dad and Mom, fourteen-year-old me, twelve-year-old, raven-haired Carrie, eleven-year-old, blonde haired, bubbly-personality Aly; we are the Warner family. My dad is a great preacher, at least I think so, and we are almost always on the go.

On our last trip to Boomer, West Virginia, an unusual thing happened, and we had a pretty good indication that it would be happening again as well. We were awakened in the middle of the night by the voice of a train conductor calling our names. That launched us into an adventure way back in the year 1912! We would be awake in the day of 1912 while asleep in our own time, and then when we went to sleep in 1912, we woke up in our own time, rested and refreshed. But what happened was real. The conductor told us that we had been chosen for this task. But he also warned us that if any of us got hurt or killed in the night-time adventure, we would be that way come morning in our own time. That would be hard to explain, so needless to say we were very careful! I ended up with nothing worse than badly bruised knuckles from pounding the snot out of a bad man who desperately needed it.

Everything ended well, though, and the little boy trapped by bad men in the coal mine was now safely back with his mom, rescued by us. Even more cool than that, my new 1912 friend, Big Jackson, whom I had brazenly introduced to sweet Miss Sarah, had gone on to marry her. I found that out by logging onto the internet and looking up genealogy records the next day. All in all, that adventure turned out to be a complete success. You really should read about it sometime, since I can't possibly tell you all about it here.

Anyway, the three of us kids had called a hasty meeting and decided that we really should have a name for our little team. After much debate, we settled on calling ourselves "The Night Heroes." We didn't know where our next adventure would take us, or when it would come, but we felt ready now that we had some experience and a cool name. What we did know was where our dad was taking us. We were heading from the high mountains of West Virginia to the flat land of Fayetteville, North Carolina. Dad would be preaching a second annual meeting for Pastor Eric Johnson and the Bible Baptist Church. Pastor Johnson and my dad had met while dad was teaching at the Carolina Bible College in Concord, North Carolina, and Brother Johnson was a student there. Pastor Johnson and Mrs. Amity, his wife, have kids... lots and lots of them! Nine, in fact, and all of them as nice as could be. We liked that, since it meant we would have plenty of people to play with during the week.

If you ever go to Fayetteville, it won't take you long at all to figure out that it is a military town. You will pass by a huge bombing range on the way in, you will share the road with camouflage covered Humvees, and you will see soldiers in uniform in almost every store and restaurant. Fayetteville is home to Fort Bragg, home of the world famous 82nd airborne division. My dad is a major military buff and has gotten me hooked on it too. He has a cannonball from the Revolutionary War, a Charlie Stick from Vietnam, and a display of bullets and Confederate buttons from the Civil War. That is in addition to all of the history books about war in his office back home. Dad always says that our soldiers are heroes, and that we need to respect them and pray for them. I have seen dad many times pay for a soldier's meal out in public. He says they aren't paid nearly well enough for all they do and all the risks they have to take. When we pray, we almost always think to pray for a Marine Corp veteran from our home church, Bobby Kramer. He has a sweet wife named Rachael, and their two kids Alex and Andrea are very good friends of ours. Mr. Bobby has been to Afghanistan for several tours of duty, and all of us look up to him.

Just off of All American Parkway in Fayetteville, we found Bordeaux Parkway, where the Fayetteville Inn and Suites is located. We stayed there last year, and Pastor Johnson had booked a room for us there again this year. It was Monday afternoon, and dad would be preaching Monday night through Friday night. We pulled into the parking lot of the hotel, and Mom went in to check us in while dad started pulling luggage out of the Yukon. Carrie and Aly and I stretched our legs, then I went and got a luggage cart. We had it loaded quickly enough, and soon we were wheeling it into the hotel. Into the foyer, turn right through the double glass doors, left, then straight on past the desk. Weave left down the hallway, and soon we found ourselves at the last room on the right. Within minutes we were unloaded and organizing everything in the room. When you do this every week, it doesn't take long for everyone to know their assigned tasks! And everyone helped in some way, because as mom has always taught us, "Many hands make light work."

We had just a few minutes to rest up, and then came the whirlwind of activity that mom calls, "Everyone get dressed for church this instant!"

Dad and I tidied and tucked, while mom and the girls powdered and puffed. Good grief, what is it with girls anyway? They put so much powder into the air it reminds me of a gardener spreading Sevin Dust on his plants to kill the bugs! When I ask dad about it, he just grins at me and says, "Trust me on this one, boy, you will understand one day very soon, and you will appreciate it." I'm not so sure.

In practically no time, we were done, loaded, and headed for Bible Baptist Church. The sign out front announced "Family

Conference this Week, Rev. Warner." That meant that my dad would be preaching about how Christian families should behave toward one another. I always like those kinds of revivals, because dad always has a lot of funny stuff to say, even though there are some things he says that I don't understand. He says he will explain it all to me when I am old enough.

The first night of the meeting went well. Dad preached a message from the marriage of Jacob and Leah called "Do You Know Who You Married?" That is a really funny story from the Bible, Genesis 29, and it is all true! A guy named Jacob thought he was marrying a pretty girl named Rachel, but he got tricked into marrying a not-so-pretty girl named Leah. Maybe she should have talked to my mom and sisters about the puffing and powdering thing; it probably would have helped.

Once the meeting was done, our family and the pastor's family and a bunch of others from the church went down to the Sonic and got milkshakes. The Sonic in Fayetteville is really cool; it actually has a massive playground! We played while the adults talked. Then before you know it, it was time for us to get to the hotel, get showered off, and get some sleep.

Getting five people ready for bed in a hotel room with one bathroom is no easy job. When you think of your favorite evangelists, pray for them! But finally we were all done, dad and mom prayed with us, and we were ready for bed. Mom and dad had one bed, the girls had another, and I had a roll-away cot. Believe me, after a long day of traveling, you can fall asleep on about anything. And fall asleep we did; fully...fast...and temporarily.

Chapter Two

It was very dark, so it wasn't light that woke us up. And this time, it wasn't a train conductor's voice calling us either that made us sit up and take notice. No, it was the unusual droning, engine-sounding noise that made all three of us sit straight up in what we mistakenly thought was bed. As it turns out, it wasn't bed anymore at all. I was laying down/sitting up on the ledge of the inside of an old military plane of some type, and Carrie and Aly were laying down/sitting up on the ledge across from me. I looked around, and as my eyes adjusted to the darkness, quickly tried to gather as much information by sight as I could. I was used to flying but only in modern jets. This was clearly no modern jet. There were no seats, nor was there the smooth whirring of any jet engines. Instead, there was the unmistakable sound of propeller driven engines clawing through the air, a much harsher sound than jet engines make. The cabin area was sparse, with just the ledges for sitting, green military boxes of some kind stacked up on each other, and a rack with what appeared to be parachutes.

Up front, I could begin to see the very dim lights of the cockpit, with the silhouette of a man at the controls of the plane.

"Well, here we go again," said Carrie. "I wonder where we are headed to this time."

"And I wonder *when* we are headed to," Aly groaned as she rubbed at her eyes.

"Those are good questions," said a very familiar voice, "and welcome to my plane."

Looking up, we realized that the pilot had left the cockpit and was standing in front of us. Smiling, we saw that our pilot for this adventure was none other than our train conductor for our last one.

"Good evening, Sir," Carrie said with a smile. "It's good to see you again. When did you move up from trains to airplanes?"

Smiling right back at her, our conductor/pilot said, "You will find that I have many skills and abilities given to me by my Boss to fulfill whatever His needs for me are. And right now, He needs me flying this plane so that you can get to your destination on time."

"Last time, our destination was a coal mine in the year 1912," I said, "and a little boy that needed our help. Where and when are we headed this time, and what are we needed for?"

With me only fourteen years old, you may wonder why I refer to anyone as a little boy. My dad has made sure that my "little boy years" didn't drag on too far into my young adulthood. Dad believes that boys should work, wrestle, tussle, work some more, and become strong and useful young men. All of that hard work and hard play has made me at fourteen more of a man than a lot of twenty year olds. I am starting to have fairly decent muscles, and dad has taught me how to fight and use them.

"Your destination is one that will be new to you. You are going to Germany. As to the 'when,' " he said as he took a deep breath, "the year is now 1943, and World War II is raging. America and her Allies are pushing back hard against the Nazis and the Axis powers, and Hitler is reacting in panic and desperation."

Gulping hard, Little Sis, Littler Sis, and I looked at each other. Wading into the middle of a coal war and fighting against a bunch of miners to rescue a little boy was dangerous enough. But this was actual war we were now talking about! I knew from history that more than fifty million people died during World War II, many of them children. Hitler and the Nazis cared nothing for human life and would kill children just as quickly as they would adults. Why were we being called into something as dangerous as this, especially when this war was over six decades or more before our time?

"I am sure that in your studies you have heard of things called concentration camps. Hitler uses them as a means to imprison, torture, and then destroy people. Most of those people are Jews, which I am sure from your Bible studies you know a great deal about."

He was right about that. Every good preacher I know preaches and teaches a lot about the Jewish people. Jesus was a Jew. The Bible was written to and by Jews. The Jews became God's chosen people, as far as nations go, way back in Genesis 12. It was there that He told a man named Abraham, "I will bless them that bless thee, and curse him that curseth thee: and in thee shall all families of the earth be blessed." Dad told us often that we are to love and pray for the Jewish people. They may not love Jesus, but Jesus loves them, and that means that we are to love them as well.

"What does that have to do with us?" asked Aly with a bit of fear in her voice. "Aren't we a bit young and unprepared to wade into the middle of World War II? There are soldiers for that; men who are trained to deal with that kind of thing."

"Yes, there are," said the pilot. "You have not been brought here to do their job; you have been brought here to do yours. Those soldiers down below are fighting and killing the enemy, and they are doing so in the perfect will of God. When evil men need to be stopped, God calls soldiers to do it. Your job is of a different nature. There is a young girl in a concentration camp, and the Lord has need of her. She will be killed in five days if she is not rescued. No soldiers know of her, and none would be able to turn their attention to rescuing her even if they did know of her. That is why you have been brought here."

"Pardon me, Sir," Carrie chimed in, "but there were six million Jews killed in the concentration camps during World War II. How in the world are we going to find one young girl? And even if we did, how in the world could we ever get her out of a concentration camp? If we did get her out, where could we go with her to keep her safe? And furthermore, how do you plan on landing this plane in the middle of Nazi Germany for us to get near a concentration camp?"

"I'm not landing," said the pilot. "You are jumping."

Chapter Three

For at least twenty seconds, we were absolutely silent, completely stunned. Finally, as the oldest present member of our family/team, I stammered and spoke, "Uh, but, uh, now, surely you didn't mean, I mean, you don't actually expect a little boy and two little girls to jump out of a plane into a war zone, do you?"

"It is interesting to hear you call yourself a little boy at this moment," said the pilot, "since you get angry if anyone else at any other moment calls you that."

I could feel my face turning red, because I knew he was right. As scared as we all were at that moment, Aly actually giggled out loud at what he said and at my red face. Brat.

"And yes, I actually do expect all of you to jump out of this plane. I will not force you to do so, no one is ever forced to do God's will.

People either do God's will willingly or not at all. But the three children that did so well on their last adventure, well enough to be called "The Night Heroes..."

As he said it and his words trailed off, all three of us turned red. We felt so awkward at that moment, but fortunately, the pilot began to laugh—a warm, comforting laugh.

"Don't be embarrassed. The name is a good one, and you earned it. But every good name must be earned and re-earned on a constant basis. Even the name 'Christian' is like that. You may live Christ-like enough today to earn that name, but today's behavior does not earn you anything tomorrow. As for your fear, it is normal. Any children your age would be scared right now. But you have shown a willingness to overcome your fears and sacrifice yourselves for others. You will need to do so again."

"But we have no idea how to safely jump out of an airplane!" said Carrie. "Even our dad has never done that. He and heights don't get along too well."

"You will not have to worry about the how," he said, "that is simple enough. Once I strap you into the chute, you will line up at the door of the plane. I packed these chutes myself, they are going to do the job. When I say 'go," you will jump out of the plane, one immediately after the other. You are hooked to what is

18

called a Static Line, meaning that you do not have to do anything other than jump, and your parachute will open. You are light enough that the chutes will carry you down to a relatively soft landing. When you are nearing the ground, bend your knees slightly, turn your toes a bit outward, and then drop and roll. Then get up quickly and hide your chutes."

"And what do we do then?" I asked. "What concentration camp are we looking for? How do we get there? Who is the girl? How do we get her out? What do we do then?"

"You will be looking for Ravensbruck," he said, and immediately I felt a chill course through my body. I remembered reading about that awful place in the book *The Hiding Place,* written by Corrie Ten Boom. It was a wicked, dark, terrible place. Ravensbruck was a concentration camp for women. It was there that Corrie Ten Boom's sweet, old sister, Betsie, had died. Unspeakable horrors had been committed in that place.

"The girl you are looking for is Miriam Lebowicz. She is twelve years old. Her mother and father have already been killed. Her grandparents are praying for her every single day. They were in America before the war began and were unable to go back home. If you can get little Miriam to them in New York, she will be safe."

I was looking toward the cockpit of the plane as he spoke and could see just the faintest hint of light beginning to touch the distant horizon. In half an hour the sun would rise, and we would need to be somewhere under cover till we could get our bearings and figure out what we were going to do. That meant that this conversation was almost over, because we were going to need to jump in a matter of minutes.

"Begging your pardon, sir," Carrie said, "but why this one little girl? Out of six million people, why her?"

"That is an excellent question, young lady. And the answer is, because of her son. You see, if she lives and escapes, she will one day get married and have a baby boy. And that baby boy, who will grow up and become an adult in your own time, will one day fulfill a very special task. Ezekiel 38 tells us that one day, many large nations of the world will invade Israel and try to destroy her. Little Miriam's son, David, will become the Prime Minister of Israel, and his leadership along with God's intervention will save Israel during their darkest hour. God has raised up Miriam to have that child, He will raise up that child to protect Israel, and He has raised up you to save her so that all of this can one day happen."

There are times when the gravity of a situation hits you like a ton of bricks, and this was one of those times. This was not just a little boy in a coal mine we were trying to save, this was literally the nation of Israel herself! If little Miriam died in Ravensbruck, there would be no David, and if there was no David, Israel would not have her needed hero in her darkest hour. This is what my dad would call "heavy." I looked over at the girls, and man, I could not have been more proud of them. Carrie had that calm, assured look about her. Aly had her typical, "I am going to gnaw Hitler's leg off like a beaver all the way up to his kneecap" kind of expression. We were about to jump out of a perfectly good airplane, and they were calmer about it than I was!

The next few minutes were a blur of activity. The pilot moved like the wind, fastening just the right sized parachute on each of us. Every cinch was tightened, and everything was explained two or three times in a row to make sure we understood it. Then he placed his hands on my shoulders and said, "That's everything."

"I don't mean to argue with you," I said, "but this is definitely not everything. We have learned to always pray before anything we try and do for the Lord, and we are going to do so now. No way are we jumping out of a plane without speaking to God about it first!" The pilot just smiled, nodded, and a split second later we were all on our knees, pouring out our hearts to the Lord.

Chapter Four

The sensation of jumping out of an airplane is difficult to describe. Everything within you is protesting the idea. God has built a survival instinct into mankind, and that very instinct has to be fought against in order to jump out of a plane. We were lined up at the door, me first, then Aly, then Carrie. When the pilot opened the door, there was a whooshing sound that filled the cabin and a massive change in air pressure. Once we adjusted to that, I got right up by the door, with the other two behind me in a line. The pilot, who would now be our jumpmaster, had his left hand on the top of the door frame, his right arm across the opening, and was looking down at the ground. Then he began to count backwards from five:

"Five...four...three...two...one... Go!"

A jump into nothingness...a split second of falling in which your stomach jumps up into your throat...then a jerk as the static line engages the parachute. After that there was four or five seconds where I was not breathing but had not yet realized that fact. Finally that breath came, in gasps. Quickly I got myself oriented and looked around for my sisters. Aly was off to my left, Carrie to the right. The plane was quickly getting smaller and smaller as it streaked away from us. Every second brought us a bit closer to the ground, and in about 10-12 more of those seconds I knew we would be down. Fortunately, the fact that we are still just kids meant that we would land fairly softly.

With three soft "thuds" we touched down. Remembering what the pilot had told us, we scrambled like crazy to get out of our chutes and get them hidden in the trees. We had landed in an open field, about a hundred yards from the tree line. That was excellent placement; far enough out in the open to land safely, but near enough to the trees to get under cover quickly. I guess it took us about three minutes to get out of the harnesses and get us and our chutes into the trees and hidden. A real airman could no doubt have done much better, but for a bunch of untrained kids, I guess we didn't do so badly.

The sun was beginning to send its first rays up over the horizon. Within a few minutes, traveling in the open would be very, very dangerous. Fortunately, the German countryside was one of forests, glades, valleys, farmland, and plenty of other places to take cover. Unfortunately, we had no idea where we were, we had no idea where Ravensbruck was, none of us could speak German, and we had no idea what to do next! For a few minutes we brain stormed (that was my part) and argued (that was the girl's part) and yet could not decide what to do. For some reason, our "discussion" actually started to get pretty heated and pretty loud! Kids should never do that. One day your brothers and sisters may not be there anymore, and you will wish you had been nicer to them. But none of us were thinking that clearly at the moment. We were each just stating our opinions, loudly, and not getting anywhere. I myself was in the midst of about a thirty-second lecture, telling my little sisters that they needed to listen to me, since I was the oldest. But would you believe it? Right in the middle of that logical lecture, Aly stomped on my foot, and then put her hand over my mouth to stifle my yell!

"Be quiet!" she told me. "Listen! Can you hear that?" Right away we all heard it. It was a very familiar sound to us, the sound of a train chugging up a set of tracks somewhere nearby. Quickly we identified the direction from which the sound was coming and instinctively ran through the trees toward it. We weren't sure what we had in mind, or even if we had anything in mind, we just knew that we had to do something, and running toward the sound of a train was something.

Within thirty or forty seconds, we pulled up panting to the eastern edge of the woods. I knew that it was the eastern side because it was facing the sunrise. There, a quarter mile or so away, chugging its way up the track, was a long train pulling a large number of boxcars. We watched it draw ever closer, wondering what would happen next. What happened then was not something that we expected or would ever forget.

Chapter Five

As the train neared our position, we realized that it was slowing down. Slower, slower, slower, slower, until finally it stopped just a little way up ahead of us, close enough that we could peek past the trees and see and hear everything that was happening.

As soon as the train came to that stop, several German soldiers, all wearing that ominous black swastika on their arms, jumped out of the train. They took up positions in a semi-circle facing it and began to shout orders that we could not understand. One of them began going to each box car, one by one, and opening the big side door. When he did, my stomach turned upside down. I could hear Carrie suck in a hiss, and I could see Aly beside me fighting hard not to get sick. Each one of those box cars were jam cram packed with women and girls, and when I say packed, I mean packed like sardines in a can. Those poor abused people blinked in the bright light of the rising sun and practically fell out of the different box cars. It took many of them several minutes to be able to stand up right; they had obviously lost circulation in their legs from long hours in those cramped conditions. The soldiers, though, were clearly in no mood for delay. I guessed that they were screaming for the women to go to the nearby creek and drink, especially when they began literally shoving them that direction. One young punk soldier shoved an old woman in the back so hard that she fell face forward onto the ground. And then he and the rest of the soldiers laughed and pointed at her, clearly enjoying seeing a helpless old woman struggling to get to her feet.

I felt a hand on my arm, and I realized that both of my fists were balled up tight, my jaw was clenched, and Carrie had her hand on me. "Easy, Big Brother," she said. "I know you want to clobber that guy; I do too. But there are at least fifty heavily-armed soldiers out there. If you go after that guy now, the only thing you will accomplish is to get yourself and us killed. Remember what the Conductor told us—our job is to rescue a little girl; the soldier's job is to kill the bad guys. Trust me, people like that don't get by with what they do forever; his day is coming."

I knew she was right. Since the time we were little our dad had quoted a particular verse of Scripture to us so very many times that it was now burned into our memory. It was Galatians 6:7 which says, "Be not deceived; God is not mocked: for whatsoever a man soweth, that shall he also reap." That means that for good or bad, you will eventually get what is coming to you, no doubt about it. Silently I prayed that God would somehow let me be the one to give that filthy punk what he had coming to him.

The women and girls were wearing tattered clothes, dirty and threadbare. They had a look of hopelessness etched onto their faces as they were marched to the creek. In large groups they were made to kneel down and drink from the muddy waters of that pitiful excuse for a creek. That water looked like something that the neighborhood dogs would turn up their noses at. But those pitiful women and girls seemed grateful for it. I wondered how long it had been since they had been given anything to drink at all. By the looks of them, both food and water had been scarce.

After what seemed like only minutes, all of them were herded back to the train and forced to load back up in the boxcars. It was then that I heard a soft sobbing sound beside me and looked over to see Aly with tears streaming down her rosy little cheeks. She was trying to speak and finally managed to get out the words, "One hundred and twenty."

"What?" I said, "One hundred and twenty what?"

"They are putting one hundred and twenty women in each of those box cars. They are going to suffocate and die in there like that. Why? Why do they have to be so mean to them? What did those innocent little girls and tiny old women ever do to them to deserve to be treated like that?"

"Nothing, Sis, absolutely nothing. They didn't have to. Those men hate them and mistreat them simply because they are Jews. Evil men have always hated the Jews. Think of wicked Haman in the book of Esther. Think of Muslims across the Middle East in our day. Think of Hitler here in World War II. The devil hates the Jews because God loves them. So he stirs up bad people in every generation to try to hurt and destroy them."

"Right," said Carrie. "But they won't get by with it. Remember the promise that God made to Abraham? It was in Genesis 12:3 that He told him "And I will bless them that bless thee, and curse him that curseth thee: and in thee shall all families of the earth be blessed." Dad says that God is still keeping that promise even today. That is one reason why America has been so blessed; she has stood with the Jewish people. And that is why Hitler is going to lose this war and his life, because he came against the Jewish people."

"But in the meantime," I said, "We have some miles to cover." We all three looked out at the train at that moment, and it was beginning to chug its way on up the tracks, belching out billowy black smoke as it picked up momentum. "When it crosses over that hill, we are going to follow it, no matter how many miles of tracks are ahead of us."

"Bro, let it go," said Carrie. "I thought we decided that you would leave that soldier to God to handle? We have to find Ravensbruck and rescue little Miriam.'

"That's why we are following the tracks, Sis," I said. "Everyone on that train was a woman or a girl. There was only one concentration camp in World War II built to house only women and girls and that was Ravensbruck. We follow those tracks, and they will lead us right to it. The fact that Punk Boy is going there as well is just icing on the cake to me."

"And how did you become such an expert on German concentration camps, Mr. Einstein?" she asked sarcastically.

"It's called 'homework,' Sis, you might want to try it sometime," I retorted.

Would you believe it? My own sister punched me in the gut and started walking. I looked over at Aly and found no sympathy at all.

"You had that coming," she said. "Now how about putting on your big-boy pants and coming along with us. We have work to do," she said as she walked away.

Girls! Sometimes I wonder if God knew what He was doing when He made them.

Chapter Six

God is good, all the time. We say that, and it is true, but it is also nice when we see it first-hand. As we began to warily follow those train tracks, we marveled at the "all the time" goodness of God. Here we were in Germany, a place we had never been, needing to follow the tracks of a train and yet needing to avoid being seen as well. We wondered how we could do that, when suddenly it got a whole lot easier. Over the very next hill, those tracks veered to the right and went straight into one of the lovely forests of Germany. I estimated it to be about a third of a mile to that point. We scanned the area, saw no one nearby, and then made a mad dash for that forest. We covered the ground pretty quickly, and we soon bent over, grabbing our knees, and gasping in large breaths of air. Finally our breathing returned to normal, and we started walking.

The forests of Germany are lovely things. Based on the vibrant colors of some of the leaves (reds, oranges, yellows, and purples), I guessed that it was the fall of the year. Trees with those colors, though, were actually in the distinct minority. The vast majority of the trees in which we now walked were very tall pines of a variety that seemed different than the typical American pine. By the preponderance of pines, I guessed that we were in northern part of Germany, since most of the hardwoods were in the south.

"Little Sis and Littler Sis," I said, "I think we may not have too far to walk. These trees tell me that we are in northern Germany. If that is the case, Ravensbruck can't be too far. If memory serves me correct, it was about sixty miles north of Berlin. A hundred miles later or so you would be all the way to the Baltic Sea. Prisoners were usually processed in Berlin and then taken to the camps. So we should be past Berlin and in one of the forests leading up to the lowlands just past Ravensbruck."

"For once I think your geography may be good, Bro," said Carrie, "I was thinking the exact same thing. Why don't we run for a bit while we have the cover of the trees to work with? How quick was your last 5k time?"

"Around 25 minutes," I said. "Can you guys keep up? Because we really need to stay together."

"You go a little slower than normal, we'll go a little faster than normal, and we'll run for a while," Aly said with a smile, "How 'bout that?"

"Deal," I said, and we took off at a steady jog.

Forty-five minutes later we pulled up and slowed to a walk. I figured we had gone maybe three and a half miles. The scenery had been lovely, with an abundance of wild life, really large ferns, towering trees, and the occasional brook. As we gathered our breath, we began to talk as we walked. We didn't know how far we had to go, or what we would do when we got there, so we just made small talk. We talked about our mom and dad, our church back home (Best! Church! Ever!), and about the Lord. As we were walking and talking, something was trying to wriggle its way into my consciousness. Finally I stopped walking, and when I did, the girls immediately did too.

"What is it?" Aly asked with a look of concern.

"That smell," I said. "I'm just now realizing that a smell has been bugging me for the last few minutes."

"Bro," Carrie said, "we've lived with you for years now; we've gotten used to the smell."

Aly started to giggle out loud at that one, but I shushed them both.

"I'm serious," I said. "For a while there, all I could smell was the beautiful evergreen trees we were walking through, like a big giant Christmas tree farm. But for the last little bit I've been smelling something else, something not natural."

Both of the girls stopped, got very serious, and sniffed the air.

"I smell it, too," Aly said

"Yeah, me too. What is it?" said Carrie.

"I don't know. It's sort of smoky but not like a house burning and not like something being cooked on the grill. I have a bad feeling about this. The longer we have followed these tracks, the stronger that smell has gotten. I think I might know now what it is. Let's keep walking; we should know very soon."

An hour later we did.

As we crested a hill, the forest suddenly stopped, and we instinctively dropped to our bellies. We crawled to the crest of the hill, looked over it into the valley below, and could not hold back a gasp. There below us was a gray, barren, concrete and barbed-wire jungle. Ravensbruck. We quickly surveyed it with our eyes. It was huge and horrible. There were several long, depressing barracks and a few nicer buildings that we figured were for the captors, not the captives. In the center of the camp there was a squat concrete building and coming out of the top of it was a tall, square, concrete smokestack. There was a thin gray smoke wafting out of it, which was clearly the source of the smell that had been bothering us. I felt something wet land on my right hand, and I realized that it was a tear, one of my tears. It had streaked down my face, hung for a moment on my chin, and then dropped into hopelessness.

"Is that what I think it is?" Carrie asked as she stared at that smoke stack.

"I'm afraid so, Sis. That is where that maniac Hitler kills those poor people when they are no longer useful to him. A lot of people lost their lives in these concentration camps. For all we know, Corrie Ten Boom may actually be down there right now. She will live through it, but her sister Betsy won't."

"What are we going to do?" Aly asked. "This isn't like the last time. Last time you just pretended to be a worker in the coal mine. And since it was normal for boys to work in the mines, no one even questioned it, you just walked right in. How are we going to get into Ravensbruck? None of us speak German, and we are all just kids. We can't just walk in, and if we did, they would never let us out."

"We need to do this time what we did last time. We need to gather as much information as we can, and then figure out what we need to bring back with us to do the job."

For hours we crawled about from place to place, tree to tree, taking in everything, desperate not to miss anything. Every bit of knowledge we gathered would be a tool to be used to accomplish our task. Finally, we pulled back into the trees a bit and went over what we now knew. The camp was immense and was designed in such a way that nothing was going to be easy. There was a set of massive iron gates, the only entrance or exit to the entire place. There were guard towers. There was a triple row of wire running all along the top of the fence, and the skull and crossbones signs on it let us know that it was electrified. Climbing over was not an option. Pushing in the gates was not an option. Truthfully, we just did not see any option; we did not see any way to get in and get a little girl out.

While I was mulling all of this difficulty over, Carrie hissed, "Look!"

I followed her finger to see the large iron gates opening up. Then I saw what looked like several hundred women and girls marching toward the gate from outside, with a handful of soldiers guarding them. They were marched in and then the gates closed behind them.

"What were they doing out of the camp?" Aly wondered aloud.

"I don't know, Sis, but we need to find out," I said. "Something tells me it could make all the difference in the world to us and maybe to little Miriam. They came up the pathway right beside that little lake. We need to work

38

our way around there and see what is over that hill that is important enough for ladies from the camp to be outside of the camp during the day."

The rays of the afternoon sun were growing long, and we knew that very soon we would have very little light to work with. We could not go left out of the trees and into the open where those ladies had come from, we would have to go all the way around the camp in the trees to the right. That looked to be at least a two-mile trek. I shook my head and laughed a low laugh. It looked like Dad was right, as always. "Work hard, play hard, push yourself," he always says. "You never know when you will need strength and endurance, and if you wait till you need it, it will be too late to develop it."

"Come on guys," I said, "Looks like we have one more run in front of us for the day. Do you think you have another two miles or so in you?"

They did. And so we found ourselves, about forty-five minutes later, on the opposite side in the trees above Ravensbruck. We eased back into those trees, down toward the lake, and found the little roadway those ladies and girls had been on. We stayed in the trees beside it and began to walk parallel to it at a brisk pace. The sun was now set, we knew we did not have much time until we had to find a spot to go to sleep in the trees for our nightly trip back to our time, and I was nervous. We really, really needed to know first where those ladies had been. Suddenly, the trees ahead of us just stopped. We had probably come a mile to a mile and a half from the camp and everything opened up. There ahead of us was a large factory of some kind. There was a sign over the main building, a sign that had one word on it, a name:

SIEMENS

"What does that mean?" asked Carrie. "I don't suppose either of you two know German well enough to translate that, do you?"

"I know exactly what it means, Sis. It means that if we are very fortunate, we may just have a way to get little Miriam out. Let's get back up into the trees, settle down for the night, and I'll explain everything."

Chapter Seven

We woke up to the droning of the air conditioner in our room at the Fayetteville Inn and Suites. We talked softly, not wanting to disturb mom and dad, who may not feel as rested as we did. How weird is that? They sleep actual sleep all night and wake up tired; we fall asleep, wake up in the past, run through the forests of Germany for hours, go to sleep there in Germany, immediately wake up back in our time, and feel completely rested. I'm glad we are a preacher's family; kids that aren't used to weirdness would probably freak out at that.

As we talked, we went over what we would need to do for the day. We knew that one thing that would be on the schedule was a trip to the Airborne and Special Ops Museum. We had been there last year, and it is incredible. It is free to the public, and before you even walk in you will be amazed. There is a huge statue called Iron Mike, a tribute to service men and women. That trip for the day would be really helpful to us, since much of the museum is taken up with displays from World War II and with information about jumping out of airplanes, which it seemed we would be doing for the next few days.

We ate a continental breakfast there in the hotel, and then we kids minded our own business and played for a while, while Dad and Mom worked on their Spanish lessons. They are learning Spanish so that they can witness to people who do not speak English. That's my folks, always concerned about others. While they were studying, I borrowed my mom's e-reader. Actually it was dad's e-reader, given to him as a gift by one of our favorite churches, Bethany Baptist Church in Thomasville, North Carolina, the first time he preached a revival there. But Mom is more of a technology person than dad, so, in his words, "he quickly lost custody of it."

I borrowed it for a specific reason. I knew that among the hundreds of books mom had on it, there was one that was going to be of extreme help to us. It was *The Hiding Place*, and my memory told me that there was some information in it that I needed. I found it, skipped toward the back, and began to read. Shortly I could hear myself saying, "Bingo..."

At lunchtime we went to Pizza Hut, which none of us complained about. Then we went on to the Airborne Museum and spent the rest of the day. Like I said, it is amazing, definitely worth the time. As we were walking through it, looking at the history of people jumping out of airplanes, I was almost amused by the fact that the Germans are the ones who did it first! But like typical Americans, we were very quickly better at it than the people who invented it.

Maybe fifteen minutes into our tour, we walked through the cabin of an old airplane. Mom and dad were impressed, but Carrie and Aly and I were stunned. This was the exact same kind of plane and cabin that we had awakened in last night! We just shook our heads and grinned, knowing that mom and dad would never be able to believe us even if we told them. A little farther on we came to a display of survival kits that were often used by airmen in the war. They would include things like a compass, some German money, maps hidden inside a pen, and mirrors for signaling any Allied planes that might be flying overhead. All of that got me to thinking that we would also need to gather some supplies for our rescue/escape mission. We learned during our last adventure up in West Virginia that whatever we have with us when we go to sleep at night, we wake up with in our adventure. I couldn't help but laugh thinking of the trauma we had inflicted on the guards at the coal mine with a laser pointer and paint ball gun!

When we were done at the museum, we went by Walmart for some supplies. Mom and dad grabbed things like Diet Dr. Pepper (Dad loves that), snacks, and Kleenexes. The girls and I got one thing of our own that I figured we might need: a compass. Everything else we might need for now I was pretty sure we had in our stuff back at the hotel.

We went on back to the hotel after that, and got ready for church and supper. Supper was at the church fellowship hall at 5:30. Like most all good churches, the folks from Bible Baptist can cook! Once we were done with supper we went on into the auditorium for service. The church kids sang a really sweet song, and then my dad preached. His message for the night was called "Law and Order." It dealt with parents and how they should raise their kids. My parents are raising us right, I know, because they do it by the Bible. It's funny how these days people are following the advice and counsel of day-time talk show hosts, magazine writers, and everyone else but God. I figure since God made the family, He surely knows how it ought to operate.

After service we went with the pastor and his family to the Dairy Queen. Complaints?

No, I can assure you, none at all. Ice cream is one of the four basic food groups, I think.

Finally it was time for us to head back to the hotel and bed down for the night. Mom and dad came over and prayed with us like they always do, and then it was down for the night. We laid there awake for a while. Since we were all in the same room, we could not move around too freely to gather our things. But after a little while we heard the soft snores of the two people we loved best in the world, and we knew we could get ready. Quietly, softly, we each reached down and grabbed three little back packs that we had put a few things in before bed, and pulled them to our chests. Then we lay there quietly, waiting for sleep–and for our ride back into the past.

Chapter Eight

If you have never heard it, the sound of anti-aircraft fire is a terrifying thing. All three of us jumped straight up, wide awake, and then were immediately thrown sideways into the cabin wall of the plane.

"Hold tight, Children," shouted out the Conductor/Pilot. "We are taking heat from gunners down below!"

Carrie and Aly dove for the ledges, grabbed hold like ticks on a hound dog, and held on for dear life. I crawled toward the cockpit, up beside the Conductor, and tried to see what was happening. There was an eerie glow from the old-fashioned dials on the console. The Douglas C-47 Skytrain we were in was rocking and shaking like a rickety building during an earthquake. I could see streaks of light racing upwards at us from the ground far below, illuminating the night sky in a garish sort of way. I looked up at the Conductor, and he had a grim, frightened look on his face. Believe me, when I saw that, I got scared too! Somehow I had figured that whatever he was, angel, ghost, or something else, that he was not able to be touched or harmed, and that we could not either as long as we were with him. But the look on his face let me know that we were very much in danger.

"Try not to worry," he said with a grim smile. "That anti-aircraft fire is not very accurate, not nearly like the computer guided weaponry in your day. Planes do get shot down from time to time, but most make it through unharmed."

"That doesn't help much, to tell you the truth," I said. "I didn't know whatever train or plane we ride on with you is actually at risk. I thought the danger didn't start till we got to our destination. I guess I shouldn't assume things."

"That is correct," said the Conductor as he veered back to the right. "You perhaps remember a verse from your Bible, Proverbs 18:13. It says 'He that answereth a matter before he heareth *it*, it is folly and shame unto him.' A short paraphrase of that is 'Don't jump to conclusions, especially before you jump out of a plane!'"

I could not help but laugh out loud at that, which brought Carrie and Aly out of hiding to find out what was going on. I quickly brought them up to speed on the new bit of information I had just learned. I figured that we would learn more and more each time we did this. Finally we were past the anti-aircraft gunners and speeding our way into the heart of Germany. I decided to take the opportunity to discuss jump plans with the Conductor, especially location.

"Pardon me, Sir," I said, "but I need to ask you about the jump site for the night. To save us some valuable time, could you possibly find us a spot to jump on the far side of Ravensbruck? That would give us some extra time to try and rescue little Miriam.

"I could," he replied, "but it would be risky. The farther we go, the more easily the enemy can guess our intentions. As you can see, just since last night the anti-aircraft gunners have set up positions to shoot at us based on where we were last night. The further we go each time, the more accurate their fire will become. If we fly you directly over Ravensbruck, they will quickly figure out that we are up to something concerning that particular camp. You would probably be best served not having me fly you over Ravensbruck until the last possible day. A few miles of running may save both your lives and hers."

That settled that, so the girls and I went back into the cabin to talk and plan. It was then that I took time to tell them what I had figured out from yesterday.

As soon as we had seen the word "SIEMENS" on that sign, I recognized it. When our home church was building the new church building, the pastor and the men of the church did it all. I helped the pastor a whole bunch; dad knew that he could teach me a great many things. The pastor and another man from church, Eddie Dennis, did all of the electrical work, and I was there to help them. We bent the conduit and pulled wires and installed outlets; it was a lot of work but also a lot of fun! But almost everything electrical that the church bought had that word Siemens on it. Siemens is one of the biggest electrical suppliers in the world. The breaker boxes, the breakers, all of it came from Siemens. That factory that we saw last night in Germany was obviously part of that company. That is why I went and scanned over the book *The Hiding Place*. I was almost sure that I remembered seeing something about it. Sure enough, here is what I read on page 200:

"After roll call, work crews were called out. For weeks Betsy and I were assigned to the Siemens factory. This huge complex of mills and railroad terminals was a mile and a half from the camp. The 'Siemens Brigade,' several thousand of us, marched out the iron gate beneath the charged wires into a world of trees and grass and horizons. The sun rose as we skirted the little lake; the gold of the late fall fields lifted our hearts."

"Wow," Carrie said with wide eyes, "do you realize what that means? We may actually see Corrie Ten Boom in that line of women! How wild is that? She has been dead for years, and we may actually see her!"

"I know, cool, isn't it!" I said with a grin. "But the important thing is, this may be the way that we can get Miriam out of there."

"What's your plan to do it?" piped in Aly. "Or is this another one of those 'genius big brother' moments where you absolutely don't have a clue?"

Feigning a hurt look, I said, "Hey, let's go easy on the sarcasm, Sis, it's not like I go off half-cocked on a regular basis!"

Man, did that open the floodgates! After four or five minutes of them ticking off a list of one item after another, I finally had to shush them so we could work through a plan. It was obvious that the first thing we had to do was to find out if little Miriam was indeed one of the girls in that huge group of women that went to work each day in the Siemens factory. If she was, we had a chance. There had been only a handful of soldiers guarding them. It was obvious why; only a handful was needed. Those poor women had been so malnourished and mistreated, they could never have run away or resisted. But that would work to our

51

advantage. We stood a good chance of freeing one little girl out of a couple of thousand if that handful of soldiers was not paying close attention.

I stretched my muscles, getting ready for the jump, which I knew was only moments away. I guess I have to admit that I liked the feeling of strength in my arms and legs. I was not a man yet, but even at fourteen I was a lot more man than I was boy.

In just a few minutes the Conductor came back to us, and without a word, the three of us rose and put on our jump packs. We also fastened our little backpacks to our sides, knowing we would need them. Then, just like the night before, we knelt and prayed, getting God involved once again in our efforts. When we were done, we all lined up, and the Conductor opened the door. We felt the drastic change in air pressure in the cabin, but quickly adjusted to it. You know, you would think that having done this once, it wouldn't be scary anymore. You would be wrong! I still remembered the feeling of my stomach jumping up into my chest last night, and I started shaking just a bit at the thought of jumping again. And then it happened...

"Can I go first?" Aly said as she nudged in front of me. "This is just too cool! Who would have ever guessed we'd get to jump out of a plane? Hey, Bro, you look a little green, you alright?"

"Uh, yeah," I answered, "I guess supper didn't sit well with me. You go ahead."

What a brat! That little munchkin wasn't scared of anything, and now I was starting to feel embarrassed.

Just a moment later, we took our second leap into the darkness, Aly, me, and then Carrie. The static line opened our chutes, and we were once again floating down through the inky darkness; down, down, down toward the dangerous land of Germany and the dangerous time of World War II.

Chapter Nine

Soon we were on the ground again. Now that we had a little experience, we were able to improve our speed over the night before. In fact, this time I timed it on my stopwatch, and we came in at two minutes and forty-one seconds to get all of our chutes and gear hidden in the woods beside the others from the night before.

"Check it out, Little Sis and Littler Sis, two minutes and forty-one seconds!" I said

Aly looked over at Carrie, seemingly perplexed, and said, "Why does he do that?"

"Because," Carrie intoned with an air of superiority, "he is a human male, and therefore has a desperate need of having his ego reinforced with meaningless demonstrations of what he perceives as his great athleticism."

"Hey, Pipsqueak," I shot back, "pipe down and show some respect. The fact that you have a superior vocabulary won't keep me from popping you upside that oversized head of yours!"

"You and whose army, Cupcake?"

"Cupcake?!?" I practically shouted. "You might not want to even use that word, cause I think your hips just got an inch bigger!"

"Ohhhhhhhhh no you di'nt!" Carrie shot back, and as she did, she rared her hand back like she was going to punch me. I got the feeling this was about to be a first class sibling brawl, but then Aly brought us back to the moment.

"Hellooooo, doofuses, have you forgotten where and when we are? Does the name Germany ring a bell? How about World War II, does that sound a little familiar? Would it be possible for my two older siblings to actually be the great examples that a young impressionable girl needs?"

Then she huffed off ahead of us and didn't look back!

"What's with her?" Carrie asked in bewilderment.

"Who knows! I'm sure we may have had moments of weirdness when we were young too," I said. Then Carrie and I quickly jogged and caught up with her, and we were off into the forest of Germany, heading down the same trail we took yesterday.

The day before, we had been somewhat cautious and slow as we went, since we did not know where we were going. Today we were able to move much faster, once again following the railroad tracks. Soon we were at the same crest of the hill, the same forest edge that we had come to yesterday. Once again we looked down into the valley below and laid eyes on the awful concrete jungle called Ravensbruck. As yesterday, the smoke stack in the center of it all was spitting out that thin gray vapor, and once again I could not help but cry a little, realizing what it meant. But tears would not help anyone, so very soon we were off into the woods again, making the two mile trek to get around to the other side. We made very good time, and before we knew it we were on the northern side of Ravensbruck, about halfway in between it and the Siemens factory.

"What are we going to do now?" Carrie asked. Quickly I explained to them what I had in mind. We would need to be incredibly careful; it just would not do at all for any of us to be caught and end up as prisoners ourselves. It would be awfully hard to explain to our parents in the morning why one or more of us was simply gone.

We knew that as it was yesterday, there would likely only be a handful of guards to watch over the women and girls trekking back down the road from the factory to the camp.

Hopefully that would make our task a little easier. We had to get a message to those ladies to see if Miriam Lebowicz was among them. If we could do that, hopefully tomorrow we could begin actual rescue efforts.

Here was the scary part; in order for this to work, we were going to have to split up. I really, really didn't want to do that, but I just couldn't think of any other way.

I left the girls on the familiar side of the road, so that they could easily get back to the rendezvous spot on the crest of the hill overlooking the southern side of the camp. I crossed over the road, got down into a little ravine where I knew I would not be seen and waited. The girls went back into the trees on the other side and waited to do their part.

After waiting for what seemed like hours, we finally heard the marching of weary feet coming down the road. I tensed up, and I mean like a banjo string pulled way too tight. Planning something like this is one thing, actually doing it is quite another. I reached into my little pack, and pulled out my part of the plan. It was a nice big string of firecrackers, the same kind people have been using for generations. I knew from experience that once I lit it, I had about fifteen seconds to be long gone. This was a plan that was going to require a little pandemonium, and then a plausible explanation. I needed the ladies to get spooked enough to run for the trees where my sisters were waiting. I also needed, when the smoke cleared, for the guards to think that some little German child had been playing an innocent joke. It is for that reason that I put a piece of paper under a rock nearby the firecrackers with one word on it: Yberraschung.

After a moment the ladies half marched and half straggled into view, with the same handful of guards keeping them in line. I let some of them pass by, knowing that they could not see me where I was. Then I lit the fuse, scrambled away on my belly into the nearby trees, and about the time I got to them I heard the firecrackers go off. Instantly I was on my feet, in the trees, running like a scared rabbit, through unfamiliar woods, hoping desperately to get around the western side of the camp and to the rendezvous spot without getting caught. More than that, though, I was praying as I ran, and I mean praying with all my heart. Not for me, but for Carrie and Aly. I was terrified that one or both of them would be caught while trying to accomplish their part of the plan. Doggone it, if either of those little rascals got caught or hurt or killed, I could never live with myself. Funny how one minute I could be fighting with them like cats and dogs, and the next minute be so very terrified that I might lose them. "Please, Lord," I prayed, "please don't let that happen." I brushed away a frightened tear and picked up the pace, knowing there was nothing I could do now but run.

Chapter Ten

Hi, this is Carrie. I'll pick the story up from here for a bit, since Kyle had no way of knowing what was happening on our side of the road. Once those firecrackers went off, exactly what Kyle thought would happen did. The ladies instinctively panicked and bolted for the trees where Aly and I were hiding and waiting. We knew that they would not get far before the guards corralled them all and brought them back. All we needed was for them to get fifteen or twenty feet into the trees, so that we could hand one our little package, and sure enough, a few of them did. The guards were shouting at the top of their lungs, trying to get everyone back in line. One or two of them were firing their guns up into the air. Some of the others were heading for the other side of the road trying to find the source of the dangerous sounding noise. In all of that panic and pandemonium, I saw just what I needed. One middle aged looking lady came within a few feet of the tree Aly and I were hiding behind. I quickly jumped out, shoved a little ball of fabric into her hand, and Aly and I took off like lightning flashes racing across the stormy sky.

I am pretty sure we have never run that fast, ever. I was scared to death. What would happen if Kyle beat us to the rendezvous spot? Would he ever stop bragging, like, ever? Guys are like that, you know.

After about fifteen minutes of all-out sprinting, Aly and I pulled up and took a breather. We slowed to a walk for just a few minutes, then took off on a steady jog. We wanted to reach the rendezvous spot before nightfall so we could all go to sleep and end up back in our beds at the Fayetteville Inn and Suites together. There did not seem to be anyone following us. That was definitely good news.

"How do you think Kyle is doing?" Aly asked almost breathlessly.

"I figure he's doing fine," I said. "For a boy, he's pretty resourceful."

"I suppose so," Aly answered, but I could tell by her voice that something was bothering her.

"What's up, Sis?" I asked as I slowed to let her get up beside me.

"Well, I've just been doing some thinking ever since our last adventure back in West Virginia. How would we ever make it if anything happened to any of us? I mean, you guys are usually irritating and obnoxious, but I love you, and I don't know what I would ever do without either of you."

"Uh, thanks, I think," I said.

"I didn't mean it that way," Aly said with a half-smile. "I'm serious. I love both of you, and mom and dad, and Uncle George and Aunt Stephanie, and cousin Marah, and all of our family. We've never had anyone close to us to die. What is it like? How do people keep on going? How do kids get up and go to school after they've had to bury a brother or sister? I would be too sad to ever function again!"

"Aly," I said, "do you remember what Dad preached on just a couple of weeks ago?" I stopped, Aly stopped with me, and I pulled my little New Testament that I carry with me everywhere I go out of my pack. I opened it to the New Testament book of I Thessalonians, the fourth chapter, and I read these words from verses thirteen through eighteen:

"But I would not have you to be ignorant, brethren, concerning them which are asleep, that ye sorrow not, even as others which have no hope. For if we believe that Jesus died and rose again, even so them also which sleep in Jesus will God bring with him. For this we say

63

unto you by the word of the Lord, that we which are alive *and* remain unto the coming of the Lord shall not prevent them which are asleep. For the Lord himself shall descend from heaven with a shout, with the voice of the archangel, and with the trump of God: and the dead in Christ shall rise first: Then we which are alive *and* remain shall be caught up together with them in the clouds, to meet the Lord in the air: and so shall we ever be with the Lord. Wherefore comfort one another with these words.

"Paul didn't say that we should not sorrow; he said that we shouldn't sorrow like those that have no hope. He said that even if any of us die, we will be reunited at the Rapture, and we will always be together. Aly, we who are saved will never be apart for more than a little while. We get to spend all eternity together! Me, you, Kyle, mom and dad, all of our family who are saved will get to be together forever. If the worst thing imaginable happens, if one or more of us don't even make it to the rendezvous spot tonight, it will still be ok."

"Thanks, Sis," Aly said as she brushed away a stray tear, "I guess I needed that reminder."

"Excellent." I said with a smile. "And now I need something. I need you to run with me, very fast. If Kyle doesn't live through today, we will get to spend all eternity with him sometime later. But if he does live through today, there is no way I am letting him beat me to the rendezvous spot."

"Carrie!" Aly said in shocked disapproval.

"I don't want to hear it, Sis," I said, "I want to hear your footsteps keeping up with mine!" And a split second later our four feet were blazing the trail back around the camp to the southern side.

We ran and ran, dodging this tree, going between those, and before we knew it we were approaching the rendezvous spot. I'm not sure why, but for some reason I did the worst thing imaginable; I got careless. That is something that is easy to do, but usually carries a pretty high price tag. I should have done as before and slowed to a walk, then gotten down and crawled the last few feet to check and make sure the rendezvous spot was clear. But, anxious to beat Kyle, (and there it is, I guess I do know the reason why I got careless!) I burst into the rendezvous spot at top speed, panting and gasping, with Aly hot on my heels.

It is amazing how fast you can put on the brakes when you find yourself staring down the barrel of a mean looking gun, held by an even meaner looking young soldier! In a split second my eyes took in and my mind processed several things. Swastika on the sleeve; so the soldier was German. Anger on his face rather than fear or questions; so he was not a newcomer to this war. Finger on the trigger; so he was ready and willing to shoot. Scar across his right cheek; so he had seen hand-to-hand combat at some point.

It did not take the soldier long to size us up, and it was clear to me what he must be thinking, that Aly and I were escapees from Ravensbruck! I did not want to for fear that I would give him away, but without even meaning to I scanned around and behind the soldier looking for Kyle, panicking, thinking that Aly and I were about to be taken to a concentration camp and would never see mom and dad again.

No sign of Kyle. But it wouldn't have done much good, because almost immediately the soldier started shouting at us in German, motioning us ahead with his gun. With no plan, no weapons, and hope quickly fading, Aly and I put our hands up over our heads, turned, and began to walk through the trees toward the daylight, toward the crest of the hill. From there it would be a walk out in the open down that hill, into the iron gates, and out of time and history. I didn't want to, but as I felt the gun nudge me in the back, urging me forward, I could feel myself begin to cry. "Oh Kyle, where are you?" I whispered under my breath, while up ahead of me I could hear Aly whispering too. But it wasn't Kyle she was calling out for in her hushed tones, it was One much greater, who surely saw what we were going through. I quickly brushed away my tears, calmed my racing heart, and joined her in that whispered prayer.

Chapter Eleven

Hi, this is Kyle, I'll pick the story up from here. Unbeknownst to Carrie, I had arrived at the rendezvous spot well before she did. I was still way faster than her. Apparently, I was also still way smarter, because I had enough sense to drop and crawl to the rendezvous spot, which allowed me to see the German soldier walking around our spot, looking at the disturbed ground. Then it happened, and there was nothing I could do about it...

Girls! What do they do with that thing between their ears? My jaw dropped like a chunk of lead when I saw them bust into our spot at top speed without even looking. They nearly ran that soldier over! If they had just done as I did, hung back in the trees and waited, the guy would probably have left on his own. Now they were his prisoners, and my mind was racing a million miles an hour to try and figure out what to do about it. I had to do something, and fast. If he got them into Ravensbruck, man, what would I tell mom and dad tomorrow morning!

I knew immediately I had to do several things, fast. One, of course, was to pray. That I could do on the run, which was the second thing I had to do. Quickly, trying my best to be like an Indian scout in the Old West, I ran noiselessly back through the trees, in a loop, praying the whole way. My goal was to get ahead of them and deal with our little problem.

The ground going down out of the trees sloped down and was in terraces. That was to my advantage. There were scrubby bushes, of a type that I was not familiar with, dotting the hillside that helped too. When I got out of the trees I dove over a terrace. I got on my hands and knees, and speed crawled toward the pathway that led down the hill. I could hear the guard shouting something at the girls, like he was annoyed with them. He probably felt like they were moving too slow. I could hear myself muttering under my breath, "Trust me, Hans, you ain't seen nothing yet. Try getting them out of the bathroom in the morning, then you'll know how slow they really are."

Quickly I got to a line of the scrubby bushes that came right up against the pathway they would be passing by. I edged completely underneath, where I hoped I could not be seen, then I reached into my pocket and pulled out a little thing I had brought with us from our day. On our first adventure in West Virginia we had learned the value of carrying things with us, things that may be able to be used in a tight situation. This particular item I had borrowed from my mom's bag before we went to sleep. Mom had always told me to take it whenever the girls and I went out for walks, and I figured this foray into Germany qualified.

Within seconds I heard the three sets of footsteps coming, and I could feel myself tensing up like a cable in knots and pulled tight. Then I saw the first set of shoes pass by, Aly's pink ones. Then Carrie's blue ones passed. Right behind that was the clomping boots of the German soldier that was pushing my sisters on down toward Ravensbruck. I could feel myself getting hot with anger as he passed; who did this jerk think he was to mess with my sisters? If I pick on them, that's life. If someone else picks on them, that's reason for me to beat him into a grease spot on the ground! But I knew that, as strong as I was at fourteen years old, trying to fight a trained, armed soldier was not a wise idea. No, I had something else in mind...

I waited about three seconds after they passed, then I quietly got out from under the bushes. Then with no hesitation I reached into my pocket, pulled out my little surprise, made three or four quick steps, and was airborne. I landed squarely on the guy's back, surprising him, and knocking him face first to the ground. And then lightning went off in his brain, eliminating him as a problem, at least for a few minutes.

Chapter Twelve

"For once, I am really, really glad to see you, Big Bro," Carrie said with a smile.

"Me too." Aly chimed in. "Whatever possessed you to bring Mom's pocket Taser along with you tonight? That was brilliant! But what are we going to do now? This guy will only be out for three or four minutes. What's your plan?"

Suddenly I was having flashbacks to our last adventure:

"Waaaaay to go big brother! Promise a crying mom we're going to find her son, lost somewhere in a coal mine, and do so without a plan! Names come to mind at this point. Not names like MacArthur or Pershing or Roosevelt, mind you, more like Goofy and Donald and Daffy."

Knowing something like that was coming again, I decided to turn the tables.

"My plan was for you two to have enough sense not to come barging in like rabid buffalos and make me have to rescue you. Since that plan didn't work out, I'm winging it. Help me drag this guy back up into the trees."

It took the three of us a whole lot of tugging and huffing and puffing, but within a few minutes we had him out of sight back in the trees. He started to come around, but another jolt from the Taser put him right back out. Working quickly, we pulled some rope out of Carrie's bag, sat the guy up against a tree, and tied him up tight. Then we gagged him so he wouldn't make noise and attract unwanted attention. It was right about then that he woke up and began to struggle and squirm and make gagged noises, clearly upset at being manhandled by three kids, and unsure of what we had hit him with that nearly fried his brain.

"Well, he's awake," I said with a sigh. "Any ideas what we should do with him?"

"I know," said Carrie, clearly angry at him for trying to make prisoners of her and Aly, "let's just go ahead and kill him like he and his buddies are doing to those poor Jewish girls and women down there in Ravensbruck." Then, to make sure that he understood her meaning even if he could not understand her language, she made a slashing movement with her finger across her throat.

Now please understand, both Aly and I knew that she didn't mean a word of it. Carrie, for all of her flaws (And she has lots of them. Remind me to tell you sometime about all the years she spent liking goofy Japanese cartoons.) is one of the most tender-hearted people that has ever lived. But at that moment, that soldier did not know any of that. He got wide eyed and began to struggle really hard against the restraints but finally realized he was not getting out.

We did have a problem, though, a big one. We knew we weren't going to kill the guy. But if we left him there, he would surely escape or be found eventually and warn everyone that we were around. That would make our task of rescuing little Miriam impossible, since everyone would be alerted to our presence. But if we couldn't kill him and couldn't leave him, what could we do, especially since we only had minutes to decide? It was already nearly dark, and we should be going to sleep very soon for our nightly trip back home to our time. And then it hit me. It was crazy...no, wait, scratch that, it was absolutely insane. Would it even work? I had no idea. But if it did, oh man, what pandemonium it would cause while solving our problem! Nonetheless, I saw no other way. Quickly I pulled Carrie and Aly aside and told them what I had in mind. Aly gasped. Carrie started laughing right out loud. Aly was completely opposed, Carrie was all in favor. Since it was two to one, we immediately set my plan in motion. Boy, oh boy, this was going to be wild!

Chapter Thirteen

We woke up to the sound of the air conditioner humming peacefully in our motel room. These trips from the past back to the present were so weird; we would go to sleep, and it seemed immediately wake up back in our own time, yet feeling as refreshed as if we had slept the entire night. But when I woke up this time, there was no yawning and stretching and slowly getting up. I was instantly wide awake and as tense as a spring. My arm was still tied, and sitting up there beside me, snoring, was our soldier! Carrie and Aly were wide awake at the exact same moment. I quickly untied the rope from me and from him, and then on cue, Aly screamed like a banshee!

In the blink of an eye everyone in that room was wide awake. Me, Carrie, Aly, a very bewildered soldier, my mom...and my dad.

My dad is pretty quick to make decisions, especially when it comes to the safety of his family. When Aly screamed, he jumped straight up out of bed, looked over as the soldier was jumping to his feet, and instantly the battle was on. My dad saw some strange guy in our room beside his children and went completely ballistic. I can only imagine what he was thinking as he took it all in; some strange man dressed like a soldier from the past somehow sneaking into our motel room and getting to his children. Oh, no, Dad was not going to have any questions to ask about that, at least not until he had eliminated the threat.

I'm estimating that it took dad about $1/36^{th}$ of a second to be completely across the room to where that soldier was standing. I, though, felt like I was seeing it all in slow motion. I saw the soldier instinctively reach down for the knife strapped to his side, but before he could get it out of its sheath my dad was there. My dad is one of the strongest men I know. He bench-presses 300 pounds, is a black belt, and is all man all the time. When he hit that soldier with a hook to the jaw it sounded like a bomb had gone off. That guy crumpled to the floor like a sack of potatoes and was lights out. His jaw was pretty much on the side of his face, and I knew dad had broken it and broken it badly. Instantly he and mom, pjs and all, were scooping us up in their arms and whisking us out of the room, making sure we were all safe.

I could not believe it had worked! We had tazed the guy one more time while he was tied to the tree, then untied him from the tree and tied his arms behind his back and tied my arm to his, then quickly gone to sleep. My guess was that somehow he would be brought back with us into our time, and that my dad would "deal with him." And what was he going to do after that? Nobody in the world was going to believe that he was even sane if he tried to tell them that he and three children had traveled through time!

The next hour after dad clocked the guy was a whirlwind of activity. The police were there trying to find out how the guy got in, and the rescue squad was there to carry the guy to the hospital, where they said he would be spending "a great deal of time" having his jaw reconstructed. They estimated that he would be eating through a straw for about the next six months, and that it would be even longer until he could speak. That was an unexpected blessing, because we would be long gone before he could start telling any "crazy stories." The police concluded that the guy had been to one of the many military paraphernalia stores in and around Fayetteville, had bought an old German uniform, snuck into our hotel room in the middle of the night, and was most likely mentally disturbed. Carrie giggled a little bit at that, and I heard her mutter under her breath, "Wait till he tells you where and *when* he came from!"

We were moved to another room shortly thereafter, since our room was now a crime scene. Pastor Johnson told dad that if he wanted to cancel the rest of the meeting and take us home to get us settled down, he could do so. The three of us kids gasped; we hadn't thought of that! If dad did that we couldn't save little Miriam! Aly quickly piped up, "We want to stay, Dad. Besides, seeing you deck that guy was totally wicked!"

Dad and mom just smiled, and mom said to dad, "Sweetie, we're ok. Let's stay. Souls are in the balance, and you've always taught us that we're safer in a war zone in God's will than in a palace outside of God's will. Besides, I agree with Aly; that was...totally...wicked!" And then she kissed him, right on the mouth. Ewwww! Why do people do that, especially my parents! Yuck!

A few minutes later we were at Bojangles. Dad has a rule: only eat at Bojangles on days that end in the letter Y. There has never been another human being anywhere more addicted to Cajun Fillet Biscuits than my dad! As we sat and ate and talked as a family, mom and dad asked us over and over how we felt, were we ok, were we scared, did we need to talk? If only we could tell them all we had been through, and all we did at nights when the Conductor called for us! This was lonely business being anonymous heroes.

We spent a little time after that touring little historical sites around Fayetteville, then, inspired by our German "friend," I asked Dad if we could go to some of the military shops. Dad was good with that, and a few minutes later we were rummaging through some pretty amazing old things. One of the things I bought raised Mom's eyebrows just a bit; a blow-up Hitler doll. Our troops used them in World War II as a bit of mockery toward "Der Fuhrer," and the Germans always hated it, especially since it put Hitler in a very foul mood. Later at a fireworks store we got the rest of what I thought I would need, a really nice, specific firework, one that I could activate with a battery remote control. Then we came back to the hotel to get ready for service. That night dad preached from chapter one of the Song of Solomon, a message he calls "The Smartest Husband in the World." Mom just watched him and smiled at him the entire time. There is definitely something weird about those two.

We went out for ice cream again after service, and a great family from the church, the Vidrines, came out with us. While we were there Carrie stopped playing in the middle of a game, came over to me and asked, "What's yberraschung?"

I smiled and quickly explained, "I looked up on the internet how to say the word 'surprise!' in German. Yberraschung is surprise."

We played and fellowshipped for a while, and then it was back to the hotel to bed down for the night. Dad checked and double checked and then triple checked the locks. Then he pulled his bed into the aisle way where anyone getting in would literally have to crawl over him to get to any of us! Seeing things like that in my dad reminds me a lot of Jesus, who put Himself in harm's way for all of us. When I grow up, I hope I can be just like my dad. I guess in a way I already am, especially in these night time missions where we try and rescue others.

Soon we were all bedded down for the night, when suddenly my eyes popped open, and a terrifying thought hit me. What if dad lay there awake all night? Did our bodies stay in bed while we went into the past or did they disappear? Would we go if dad didn't fall asleep? Fortunately, I quickly found that I didn't need to worry about that. Good old dad started snoring, and I kid you not, mom joined in harmony. Good grief, those two are mushy even in their sleep!

Chapter Fourteen

Once again we were awakened to the sound of anti-aircraft fire, this time even closer than the night before. Once again the girls dove for cover under the ledge, and I crawled up into the cockpit.

"It seems our friends down below are getting more accurate," the Conductor said grimly. "That complicates things. You and your sisters better buckle up and hold on tight."

We did so, quickly, and the next few minutes felt like riding a roller coaster. An old, rickety, shouldn't-still-be-in-service kind of a ride, worse than the ones at the average county fair. I felt certain that at any moment we were going to be blown to bits, whether any of the anti-aircraft fire actually hit us or not!

Soon, though, we got through and things settled down. The Conductor came back into the cabin to see if we were ok, which we quickly assured him we were. But then his face changed, as he got a combination stern/amused look on his face and said in a professorial type of voice, "And now, Night Heroes, why don't we talk about your little escapade from last night..."

Well, come to find out, it isn't exactly acceptable for us to be snatching people from the past and dragging them into our present/ their future. The Conductor gave us a little lesson on all of the horrible things that could result from our doing so, and it sounded a whole lot like a "time/space continuum lecture" from a bad episode of Star Trek!

"I have been told to inform you," he said, "that you are not to do so again. Are we completely clear on that? You are also not to interact with any figure from the past that you may happen to recognize in any way that will alter the events of their lives. Are we clear on that as well?"

All three of us immediately answered as polite children should, "Yes sir!"

He turned to make his way back into the cockpit. As he went, though, I could hear him laughing a little and mumbling to himself, "No sir, I have never seen that one, that is certainly a first! When even the angels are laughing, you know something unique has happened..."

"Way to go, Big Bro," Carrie said with a grin, "get us sent to the principal's office on only our second mission!"

Aly just shook her head, and I just hoped the girls would both be a little more careful from now on so I didn't have to do any other ridiculous kind of thing!

Soon it was jump time, and for the third night we knelt in the cabin of the plane to pray, then stepped out onto nothingness for a slow descent into the darkness of war-torn Germany. The day before, when we had caused the panic that led some of the ladies to run into the trees, Carrie and Aly had quickly pressed a small piece of fabric into a lady's hand. It was a small scarlet colored cord with the name "Miriam Lebowicz" written on it, along with the words "Joshua 2:18"

"I hope she understands it," Aly said breathlessly as we packed our chutes up and ran for the cover of the trees. "It isn't very specific."

"She will," I answered with more confidence than I really felt. "Every Jew knows the story of Rahab and the scarlet cord. When Rahab hung that cord in her window as the Israelites were getting ready to fight against Jericho, it was a sign as to which house she was in, and that she and that house were to be kept safe. Miriam may not know exactly what is going to happen, but she will know to have that scarlet cord visible as she comes back to Ravensbruck from the Siemens factory tomorrow."

"If she's even in the group that goes," Carrie said with a grunt as she wrestled her stuff under some low hanging pine boughs.

"She has to be, Sis, she just has to be. Because if she isn't, I have no idea how we're going to rescue her."

"Do you have any idea of how to rescue her if she is?" Aly asked.

I just grinned a little and said, "I think our plans to get her away from those guards will work, but as to how to get her out of the area, out of Germany, and into America, no, not really. Help me think, and help me pray about that. And now, let's run; we don't have any time to lose."

As we ran I was thinking of all of the things I was counting on, any one of which could be disastrous if I was wrong. One, I was counting on the disappearance of the soldier being written off as desertion. I knew from history lessons that by this point in the war many German soldiers were bailing out and running toward the mercy they hoped to receive from the Allies. They certainly knew they could expect none from Hitler if they failed him in anything. Two, I was really counting on the bad guys buying my "yberraschung" as the harmless prank of a little German kid. If they didn't, there would be extra guards on hand today, and that would not be good, not in the least. Three, I was hoping they would not tie one and two together, otherwise, they would definitely be on high alert!

We knew the route well by now and were really getting good at covering the distance quickly without much huffing and puffing. We knew we had to be in place early, because we had some preparations to make before the Siemens crew got to the spot where we had our rescue planned. Fortunately we encountered no surprises or problems along the way.

Once we were in place on the northern side of Ravensbruck, we picked a spot where I thought my plan would have the best chance of working. It was in the bend of the road, where the path passed hard beside the tree line. Across the way the ground sloped sharply away down a grassy hill, which went downward for about 300 yards before it ended at the tree line on the other side. I went down to those trees, taking a section of strong rope with me. I also had some thin metal wire with me that I had taken from dad's tool box in the trunk. Carrie and Aly were right behind me and were almost done blowing up the Hitler doll. When they finished, I tied the rope in a noose around his neck, then I wound the wire around the strands of the rope. I didn't want anyone to be able to simply cut through the rope quickly, and the wire would keep that from happening. Then I climbed a tree right by the tree line, clearly visible, and tied the rope around a branch, ten or twelve feet above the ground. We now had a hanging Hitler that someone was going to have to take the time to climb a tree and get out.

Once that was done, we set the firework in place, just eight or ten feet away from the hanging Hitler doll. Then we ran back for the road, crossed back over into the trees and waited. Neither the doll nor the unfired firework were visible from that distance. But once we activated it, it would be seen for miles.

After another half hour or so, we heard footsteps coming down the road, and we prayed very, very hard. If Miriam was not there, if she was not wearing the cord, if she was not on our side of the road... there were just so many things that could go wrong, and in order for this to work, everything had to go right.

Within seconds they began to pass by, the same assemblage of weary looking eyes, the eyes of daughters, mothers, grandmothers, and even great-grandmothers. They looked as if they had no hope and were just waiting to be released by death. One after another they came, wearing drab gray prison garb, gray, gray, gray, more gray, gray, gray, and then I saw it! Coming right toward me in the sea of gray was one little strand of scarlet, our little cord hanging from the neck of a precious looking little girl. She had hair as dark as Carrie's, skin as tan as my dad, and despite the torment of life in a concentration camp, she had a look of defiance and determination on her face. Yes, I could see why she would be chosen to be the mother of the future Prime Minister of Israel. If her son had half the determination that she clearly had, he would be a force to be reckoned with in Israel's darkest hour.

Nearer and nearer they came. I knew we would need to time everything just right. Thirty feet away...Twenty...Fifteen...Ten, and I pressed the button. Two seconds later a boom went off, and all eyes turned away from the trees and up into the air across the way, a split second later and the sky was filled with a beautiful American flag firework! Friend, that got every one of those soldiers' attention. Immediately they ran down the hill toward the detonation sight, leaving only one to guard all of those ladies and girls. And it was in that moment while every eye was looking away that I reached out from behind the tree, directly behind little Miriam, put my hand over her mouth and yanked her back into the trees.

Chapter Fifteen

Quickly I spun little Miriam around to face my sisters, and they motioned for her to be silent. Seeing them, she seemed to instinctively know that we were there to help, not to hurt her. Immediately we started to run, all of us, with my hand holding tightly to Miriam's, and Carrie and Aly close behind us. We ran north, not south, and we ran as fast as our feet could carry us. We didn't stop for at least three miles. Bless her heart, little Miriam, as badly malnourished as she was, kept up with our every step. She seemed to be driven by an inner power born of desperation to never to return to that awful place. Finally could go no further, and we collapsed from sheer exhaustion and rolled under some low-hanging pine boughs. No one said anything for three or four minutes, we just struggled to regain our breath. Finally, a voice spoke. Not mine or Carrie's or

Aly's, but a brand new voice. It said one word, a question: "American?"

Her voice was surprisingly calm and pleasant. And then it dawned on me that she had spoken in English! I answered her question, "Yes," and then asked one of my own. "You speak English?"

"Yes," she answered. "My family spent a year in Great Britain when I was younger. I still have cousins there, and we spoke often by phone before the war began."

"You also have family in New York, do you not, grandparents?"

Her eyes grew wide at my question, and she asked, "How could you know that?"

"We have, uh, intelligence sources," I said.

"Is America so low on help that they are sending kids as intelligence agents into Germany?"

Aly laughed at that and said, "I like her; I think we are going to make good friends."

Looking at her again, I was just amazed by her composure. It was going to make our job much easier, I thought. Of course, making "impossible" much easier only brings it up to the level of "unlikely" when you get right down to it.

"Listen," I said, "I can't tell you where we came from or why you were picked for us to rescue. What I can tell you is that by now, even accounting for the extra time it will have taken them to cut down a surprise we left for them in the trees, the guards are likely in the process of counting the prisoners, and soon they will know that you are missing."

"You are correct," she said. "The counting process takes about twenty minutes. Once it is established that one prisoner is gone, it will take about another half hour to figure out which one. Then the area where you caused the scene and grabbed me from will then be searched, that will take another couple of hours."

"Then we need to move while we can," I said, "and put a great deal of separation between us and them. We are going north, toward the Baltic Sea. It is approximately sixty miles and one way or the other we need to cover that distance in the next seventy-two hours."

No one asked any questions, we just took a sip of water from a plastic bottle and then got up and ran. We could not possibly cover the distance on foot, but we knew that as we give our best efforts, God has ways of making up the deficit. So we ran.

My plan was relatively straightforward. We knew we had to get Miriam to safety in New York. Now I also knew that she had family in Great Britain, and that helped us. I intended to get her to the Baltic Sea and from there onto a boat for neutral Sweden. From there she could secure passage to Great Britain and from there across the Atlantic to New York.

We ran through the day, stopping to walk periodically. By the end of the day I estimated we had covered ten of the sixty miles we needed to cover. More importantly, we had put enough distance between us and Ravensbruck that no search was likely to find us. If we could just stay out of sight as we traveled, I was pretty sure we could do this.

With the sun going down, It was time for us to part with Miriam for the night. This was likely to be tricky. We needed her to sleep, while we disappeared, and then we needed her to be right there waiting for us the next day. We had arrived at a spot beside a decent sized lake, and I figured we could find it again pretty easily.

"Miriam," I said, "I need you to do something. My sisters and I are going to get you all the way to the Baltic Sea. But at night there are some things we need to do, and we need you to be waiting for us in the same spot the next day. Please stay here under these trees, get some sleep, and trust my sisters and me to be back here tomorrow morning. Can you do that?"

"As Rahab waited for her deliverers," she grinned, "I shall wait for mine."

We grinned right back, left her under the trees with a blanket from my pack and some water and snacks, and we made our exit. We went no more than 500 yards away, well out of sight, and bedded ourselves down for the night. We lay there awake for a little while, quietly talking and planning, and somewhere in the midst of all of that we fell asleep.

Chapter Sixteen

Once again we awoke in our own beds in the hotel room in Fayetteville. That began our typical morning whirlwind rush of showers, teeth-brushing, hair fixing, and the like. We ran to Bojangles for brunch, since dad seems to have an addiction to Cajun Fillet Biscuits. From there we went to a cool nature park, the Arnette State Park, with Pastor Johnson and his family. We played Frisbee golf, and man, was that cool! There are different size and weight Frisbee discs (drivers, chippers, and putters) that you use depending on how far you need to throw. There are baskets with chains, and the goal is to throw those Frisbees into the basket in as few "strokes" as possible. The course was beautiful, meandering beside the river, and then out into large old stands of trees that looked like they have been there since the dawn of time.

We played till about 4:00, then went back to the hotel and cleaned up. Then it was on to church. Dad preached on "The Restoration of a Broken Home" that night. There were lots of tears and lots of people praying at the altar afterwards. Then we finished up and went out for more ice cream and more fellowship, then back to the hotel. I was already getting tense, thinking of the daunting task that lay ahead of us. How would we cover the needed distance in time once we got back to little Miriam? And for that matter, would she still be there?

We all said our prayers, hugged and kissed everyone good night, and then it was off to sleep. But this was a troubled sleep, a painful sleep, it seemed that in my dreams my ears were hurting. I woke up, covered both of them with my hands, and looked across the cabin of the plane at Aly and Carrie, and both of them were doing the same. It only took me a second to figure out what was going on; we were flying much higher than the previous three nights. In fact, we were right that minute still climbing—and climbing fast. I made my way into the cockpit with Carrie and Aly on my heels.

"Good evening, Mr. Conductor. Why the big change in altitude for the night?"

He spoke back over his shoulder to me, "The gunners down below seem to be narrowing down our course. I am having to fly much higher just to avoid their fire."

"I understand," I said, and then added "danger or no, we need you to fly us over Ravensbruck tonight and drop us about 10-12 miles on the far side of it, otherwise we have little chance of getting Miriam to the Baltic Sea on time. We have fifty miles or so to go and only two days to do it in."

"I see. Then we will simply have to take our chances," he said with a grim smile. That began another adventurous component to the flight. We basically flew high over Ravensbruck, and then dropped like a stone as we got past it. This was going to be a far trickier jump than previous nights. The Conductor would have to stay at the controls, since he was trying to get the plane down to the right jumping altitude on time. That meant the three of us would have to handle the jump preparations and then the actual jump on our own. Without a word we went to work, and worked fast. We buckled everyone in, checked each other's gear, and then knelt and prayed:

Dear God, please protect us as we jump into the darkness again tonight. Please let little Miriam be there waiting for us where we left her. And please, please make a way for us to be safe, yet cover the needed distance on time. We pray all of this for the sake of your people,

Israel, and because of the blood of Jesus that has made us Your children, amen.

A moment later we all stepped out into the darkness and one by one floated to the ground.

When we landed, it was about a half a mile from where we had gone to sleep last night—a very good location. We quickly gathered up our chutes and dragged them into the trees, hid them all well, and then went looking for Miriam. In about ten minutes we found her, wide awake and ready to run. And run we did. I was grateful for these old forests of Germany, with trees big enough to hide people, but far enough apart to allow us to run through them at top speed. With Miriam in tow we were not able to go as fast as I would have liked. Bless her heart, she was doing her best, but months of mistreatment in that concentration camp had really worn her down. Nonetheless she pushed on like a good little trooper, and we encouraged her all we could.

Just about noon, the forest through which we were running began to thin out, and then abruptly came to an end. We got down on our stomachs, crawled up to the edge of the tree line, and looked down into a valley below. There we saw a decent sized old town, in fact, it was actually a very big old town. It was one of those sprawling things that was obviously hundreds of years old and had just sort of expanded outward like a grandpa's stomach does through the years.

"Bro, this is a problem," Carrie said. "We're sort of on a tight schedule, and if we have to go around that town, we are going to lose hours and hours of time that we don't have. What are we going to do?"

I was silent for just a second, then I heard myself saying, "Arise, go into the city, and it shall be told thee what thou must do." I shook my head and whispered to myself, "Where have I heard those words before?"

Apparently I whispered louder than what I realized, because Carrie answered, "From Acts chapter nine, where Saul of Tarsus was confronted by Jesus on the road to Damascus. When Saul asked Jesus what he was supposed to do, the Lord told him 'Arise, go into the city, and it shall be told thee what thou must do.' Why would the Lord have brought that to your mind?"

It was then that Miriam spoke, and when she did we saw that we might have a bit of a problem.

"I don't think the Lord had anything to do with that. The story of Saul is from what you call the New Testament, and it is all about the Jew called Jesus that pretended to be the Son of God. But He was an imposter, a fake, and the story of Saul isn't true."

I saw a look of mixed hurt and anger come across Aly's face. We were here to rescue this girl and now she was insulting our Jesus, the One Who called us to help her in the first place! I started to speak up, but Carrie beat me to it, and she did so with such grace and ease that even I was amazed, "Miriam, that Jesus that you don't yet believe in is the very reason we are here. He is the one that called us to come and to rescue you, because He loves you. Saul didn't believe in Him either, but Jesus has a way of making believers out of non-believers. We aren't going to badger you about Him, but I am going to insist that you do at least one thing for us: pay attention. If Jesus spoke to my brother's heart using the words of Acts chapter nine, and if He intends us to go down into that town, then I promise you there is a very good reason for it. If you pay attention, I promise you that you will be amazed, and that you won't be able to keep from believing."

Miriam pursed her lips at that but said nothing. And so, with little choice, we said a silent prayer, stepped out into the open, and walked down the hill toward the town.

Chapter Seventeen

There was apparently nothing odd about four rag-tag looking kids walking into this quaint valley town in northern Germany. It had a really unique mixture of the old and the new, even though to us it was all old! There were farmers walking cattle to market, vegetable and fruit vendors lining the streets, and then shiny new cars bustling about in the midst of it all. There were ancient grandmother types who looked as if they were around when dirt was brand new, and then the next person over we would see a young soldier strutting about in his Nazi finest.

It was the soldiers that had us the most concerned, though we knew that anyone in the town could be our undoing. Not even sure why we were there, we simply mulled about and waited for the Lord to give us some kind of guidance. I knew that we now had two huge tasks, rather than just one. We had to get Miriam to safety, but we also had to let her see Jesus in us, so that she could come to believe in Him! I thought of how awful it would be for her to be rescued in body but lost spiritually. That thought burned in my heart like a piece of hot metal, and I prayed that we could both rescue her and win her.

Presently we rounded a corner, still not sure where we were going, and came into what was obviously the town square. There was a fountain in the middle of the open area gracefully spitting water in streams up into the air, a peaceful scene standing at odds with the war raging all around and the concentration camps spitting gray vapor into the air just a few miles away. We sat down on some of the benches laid out in a circle around the fountain and rested our weary feet. We knew we ought to be going, we knew there were many miles ahead of us, but we also knew that God had told us to come down into this town. And so we waited, watched, rested, and listened.

We listened! Thank God we listened! I nearly shouted out loud. In fact I had to clamp my hand over my mouth to keep from doing so. All three girls looked over at me like I had lost my mind, and I could just imagine why. There I was turning red with excitement, hand covering my mouth, legs bouncing up and down, yes I must have looked quite a sight!

"Uh, Kyle," said Aly slowly, "if you need to figure out what the German word for 'bathroom' is, you better do so quickly."

"Shush!" I said, "And listen!" As I said that last word I motioned with my head toward the other side of the fountain to where three men were sitting, talking. They were speaking German, so I could not understand their words, but there was one word the other two kept saying to the first one that I did know: Bonhoeffer. When Carrie and Aly heard that word, they gasped right out loud. Miriam may have heard it too, but if she did she had no idea what it meant, so she just stared at us blankly.

"Bonhoeffer! Do you think it could really be him?" Carrie whispered to me.

"There's only one way to find out," I said. "You guys stay here while I mosey around the fountain."

Very casually I got up, stretched as if lazy and tired, and began to saunter around toward the other side of the fountain. When I passed by the three men, they were in obviously intense conversation, and did not appear to notice me at all. That gave me the chance to take a really good look, and when I did, my jaw must have dropped nearly to the ground in amazement. There, seated with two other men, was a man with an unmistakable face. It was a very serious face, the face of a man that looked to be in his mid-thirties. He wore round, wire-rimmed glasses, his hair was thinning, and parted over to the right. He had a dimpled chin, and piercing eyes. I had seen his face dozens, maybe even hundreds of times in my dad's library on the cover of the book with the one word title: *Bonhoeffer*. This was the famous preacher and theologian in Germany that had masterminded an attempt to assassinate Adolph Hitler. This was the man who dared to defy the establishment and who spoke up for the Jewish people when doing so would cost him everything! This was the man who was killed by Adolph Hitler. But not yet. Because now, here in 1943, he was sitting in front of me.

I knew that these two men with whom he was speaking were either some of his ministry students or some of his co-conspirators.

I walked the rest of the way around the fountain to where the girls were waiting and took my seat again. "Guys," I said, "you are just not going to believe this. It's him; it's actually THE Dietrich Bonhoeffer!"

Carrie and Aly shook their heads in wild-eyed disbelief, but Miriam just stared blankly, having no idea what any of this meant. "Miriam," I said with a smile, "that man is without a doubt the reason the Lord had us come down into this town. Dietrich Bonhoeffer is a Christian preacher, a German who is standing against what Hitler is doing. He will eventually be killed for it."

"And how do you know that?" she asked.

I gulped, Aly gulped, Carrie gulped. Quickly I regained my wits and said, "It's inevitable. Hitler will never let a man like him live."

"Well how do kids from America know a German preacher?" she persisted.

Quickly I changed the subject. "It really doesn't matter how we know him. What does matter is that I know where he is going. He spends a lot of time in Sweden, and from here he will doubtless be heading to the Baltic Sea for just that purpose. And one thing I do know is that he won't be walking there. Assuming he is heading out today, we go where he goes, and we will get you to safety."

"And how are we going to do that?" she asked with a smile. "If he drives a car we can't exactly ask to tag along, and if he takes the train we can't afford tickets!"

"Miriam," I said, "you are going to find out that our God leads one step at a time, and where He guides, He provides. Just keep doing what Carrie said; keep paying attention. It is not a coincidence that in all of Germany we just happened to run into the one person we would recognize, and it is not a coincidence that we happened to overhear people speaking his name. Trust me, you are in good hands. The way will likely be dangerous and frightening, but all four of us know what David said about that in Psalm 23, 'Yea though I walk through the valley of the shadow of death, I will fear no evil for thou art with me.'"

We all quoted that last part together. Then we smiled, sat back, and simply waited.

Chapter Eighteen

After about fifteen minutes the two men with Mr. Bonhoeffer got up and left, and he remained seated. I could tell that he wanted to give them a bit of time to go their way, and then he would get up and go his. One couldn't be to careful in this time and place. Finally he got up too, and nonchalantly began to walk. When he did, we got up too and began to follow from a safe distance. He looked around and back from time to time, but each time he did he looked right over or past us. Four kids were obviously of no concern to him; he was looking for soldiers or Gestapo.

After a six or seven minute walk, he and then we rounded a corner to the left, and when we did I saw the most beautiful sight. There before us was a train station with tracks headed north! There was a steam engine at the front of the line and behind that a bunch of carriage cars.

This was a passenger train, a common method of transportation in all of Europe, especially Germany. In fact, trains and train tracks had been at the heart of the conflict in World War One, but that is another story entirely.

I knew that if there was some way we could get onto that train, we could ride in style while getting Miriam to her destination. But how to get on board?

And then I saw him, the young, obviously drunk German soldier. He was flashing around a wad of German money, and I guessed that he had just gotten paid and was on leave. He must have come to the town to show off and to party. So here was a guy who was making money off of killing good people and stealing people's lands and homes. I supposed that would make what I was about to do ok. Ok or not, I was going to do it–and enjoy it!

"Girls," I said, "I need you to wait right here for just a few minutes, I am going to get us the money for four train tickets," I said with a determined grin.

"How is he going to do that?" I heard Miriam ask as I turned to walk away.

I heard Aly answer, "I'm pretty sure I know, and I'm also pretty sure that a punk Nazi is about to have a very bad day..."

I followed Fritz (my pet name for him) from a distance, waiting for my opportunity. Finally he walked into some kind of a general store/hotel, and I walked in behind him. He made his way through the lobby, and then entered a door with a sign and a picture on it. The word I did not recognize, the picture I did. Men's room. I smiled and walked in a few seconds after him.

A moment later I walked out, put the taser back in my left pocket, and a handful of German cash in my wallet. Fritz was on the toilet, with a nasty burn on his buns from where I had zapped him from underneath the stall wall. Between the booze and the taser, I figured he was going to be out cold for quite a while, and he would have a lot of explaining to do if anyone found him like that. I walked back through the town to the train station to where the girls were waiting. "Problem number one solved," I said as I showed them the money.

"How did you get it from him?" Carrie asked.

"Oh, I just took a 'pot shot' at him, but that's all 'behind' us now," I said, and then I laughed hysterically at my "bun puns." Miriam just looked over at Carrie and Aly quizzically.

"Don't worry," Aly said, "we never understand him either."

"Ok, look," I said, "play time's done. We have the money, now we need to get four tickets to wherever Mr. Bonhoeffer says he is going. When he gets in line, we get in line behind him, we listen to what he says, and then we wing it."

"Wing it?" said Miriam. "Is that an odd way of saying 'fly by the seat of our pants?'"

"Something like that," I said. "Look! There he goes! Everyone fall in behind him."

And so we did. People crowded around, forming a sort of line, handing money to the ticket agent, receiving tickets, and then boarding the train. Within a few moments Mr. Bonhoeffer was at the ticket gate, and we were behind him. He said just a couple of words, and I quickly memorized them. When he got his ticket and turned to the left and walked toward the train, I quickly said the exact same words he had said and then held up four fingers. There was an awkward pause, and for a moment I did not know if this was going to work. But then the lady pounded her stamper down four times, said something that I figured had to do with money, and I handed her everything I had that I had taken from the German soldier. She rolled her eyes, handed me a bunch of it back, and then gave me change from the one bill that she kept. She mumbled something in German, and I was pretty sure it would have translated to, "What are they teaching kids these days; they can't even do simple math anymore, people are lucky that I am honest..."

Shortly she handed us four tickets, and we followed in Mr. Bonhoeffer's steps to where he had boarded the train. We handed our tickets to the attendant, and he tore them in half, kept his half, and gave us the remaining half. We each put a piece in our pockets so as not to lose them, and then we boarded the train. We looked around, and there did not seem to be any numbers on any of the seats, so we figured they were first come, first served. We made our way back to the next to the last car, passed Bonhoeffer, went about three more rows, and then sat down. Carrie and I sat in the two seats on the right, Aly and Miriam sat across from us on the left.

Within a few minutes we experienced a familiar sensation, the chug, chug, chugging of the train wheels as the train clawed its way foot by foot up the track, gaining momentum as it went. It felt like West Virginia all over again. I looked over at Carrie, and she was already napping. Then I looked to my left over at Aly and Miriam, and saw a sight that I will never get tired of. Littlest Sis had her Bible out, and was showing verses to Miriam. That kid is a soul winner of soul winners, and I figured Miriam was in very good hands. So I leaned back and closed my own eyes for a minute, said a silent prayer for Aly's success, then opened my eyes, pulled my Bible out of my pack, and read for a few minutes. But only a few minutes, because I quickly fell asleep, Bible still clutched firmly in my hands.

Chapter Nineteen

"Young man, you need to wake up," a voice whispered into my ear, a voice speaking very good English but with a thick German accent. Startled, my eyes popped wide open, and I looked up into the face of Dietrich Bonhoeffer. I was scared, bad, and didn't know what to say, so I said nothing.

"Soldiers are about, and they seem to be looking for an American lad that they say robbed one of their friends. I don't see how it could possibly be you, but it is very clear that you are American, since you are holding a King James Bible in your hands. That alone is enough to attract you a great deal of attention that I am certain you do not want."

I still said nothing, but I quickly looked to my right and then to my left, and all the girls were present and accounted for. Seeing me make that motion, Mr. Bonhoeffer's eyes grew wide, and he said, "So it is you! They are saying the boy that robbed their friend boarded this train with two or three girls. Young man, I am no friend of the Nazis, and for that you may be grateful. But I cannot do anything to help you here, all I can do is give you the warning and a piece of advice. Get off this train and get off this train now. The soldiers are searching from front to back, so it will take them four or five minutes to get here. Before they do, you need to get to the back car, step out the back door for some air, and then jump from the train. I know that is a frightening thought to children as young as yourselves, but you must do it."

"Sir," I said to him with a smile, "it is not nearly as frightening as many of the other things that God has asked us to do. Thank you for your warning, and Godspeed to you."

With that, the four of us got up from our seats and walked toward the back of the train, and somehow I knew that we would never see Bonhoeffer again. I remembered the warning of the conductor and so I did not ask Mr. Bonhoeffer to take care of Miriam for us. This was our task, we were not allowed to alter his life by asking him to do it.

As we exited the back door, we could see the tracks ever fading away behind us, one clickety-clack at a time. The sun was setting in the west. Peering around the train up toward the front I saw lights from a distant town, and I smelled the salt air of the Baltic Sea. I smiled, turned to the girls and gave them some instructions, and one by one we swallowed our fear and jumped from the train like cowboys in an old western movie.

Poor little Miriam got the worst of it, she ended up with a badly sprained ankle. The rest of us got scrapes and bruises, nothing major. We all got up, and as quickly as we could hobbled into the cover of the trees, with Miriam draped between Carrie and Aly for support. We went a hundred yards or so back into the trees, getting well under cover. We could not be more than a mile from the port city by the Baltic Sea. We could not finish the job today, but Lord willing we could do so tomorrow, on day five. We knew that Miriam only had five days to live if she had not been rescued from the concentration camp, but during our last flight with the Conductor we had learned something else. When our time in our location for Dad's revival was done and we left town, we could not come back to our past location. He said it would be like that each and every time. So if we did not finish the job before we left for the next meeting, whomever we were sent to help would be on his or her own. We knew we couldn't leave this precious girl alone, she would surely be captured and sent back to Ravensbruck.

As we did the night before, we got Miriam bedded down and then explained to her that she would need to wait for us. She seemed much softer toward us now, and so I boldly asked if we could pray with her before we left.

"You may," she said. "I am not yet convinced of your Jesus, but I cannot deny that something amazing happened back in the town, with you being led to a man you recognized. That sounds amazingly like many of the things that happened in my Holy Book, what you would call the Old Testament. You may pray for me, yes, you may pray for me."

And so we did. We poured out our hearts to God under the cover of the trees of the forests in Germany of World War II. We prayed for God to keep Miriam safe while we were away, we prayed for God to bring us back to her safely in the morning, we prayed for Him to give us guidance to complete our task of getting Miriam onto a ship for safety. Above all, we prayed that our Jesus would make Himself known to her just as fully and convincingly as He did to Saul on the Damascus road.

And then we turned and walked away a half mile or so, bedded down for the night, prayed yet again, and went to sleep.

Chapter Twenty

When we woke up for our last day in Fayetteville, we carefully covered our scrapes and bruises from our jump from the train, and got going with our day. Dad wanted to go back to the Airborne/Special Ops Museum one last time, and I was all in favor. So after our breakfast (Bojangles, are you surprised?) we headed on down there. Mom and Dad took pictures of us with big Iron Mike. Then we went inside and watched the airborne history video. We toured the entire place as we had earlier in the week, and we kids especially just drank everything in. We spent a lot of time looking at the displays and videos of actual free-fall parachuting.

"Aren't you glad we aren't having to do that?" Carrie said with a grin when mom and dad were out of earshot. "Just jumping with the static line is scary enough!"

"I'll say!"

"Me too," echoed Aly, "although, you know, it might actually be kind of cool to try!"

"Bite your tongue, Twerp," I told her. "As sure as you say something like that, we'll end up having to do it, and I am not good with that, not at all. So retract that thought and move along."

A little while later we were at a little Mexican restaurant just down the road for lunch. I think mom may actually be part Hispanic, because she could literally eat Mexican food three times a day. Our table was filled with fajitas, burritos, chips, and salsa. We ate, we laughed, and we prayed for the last night of the meeting. In spite of the fact that we kids were engaged in a life or death struggle for the life of a little girl each night, our entire family was engaged in a Heaven or Hell struggle for the souls of men each night. We had one more night to see souls saved and families helped, and so we prayed.

Once lunch was over, we hustled back to the hotel and got cleaned up and dressed in our church finest. Funny, a lot of churches these days have adopted a "come casual" approach to church. But I wonder, if none of those folks would go to the White House to see the President in casual clothes, why would they go to the House of God to meet the King of Kings that way? Maybe I'm just too young to understand, but believe me, nobody in our family was going to go to church in anything less than our best.

Church that last night was really good, we laughed a lot and cried a lot, and I saw husbands and wives sitting closer to each other than they had at the beginning of the week. After a family conference Dad always says something along the lines of, "Well, if the pastor has to expand the nursery later this year it has been a good meeting." I'm not sure exactly what he means, but mom always elbows him when he says it.

After the meeting we had one more time to fellowship over ice cream, and we did. Pastor Johnson and his family and church folks are so sweet, we just hated the thought of leaving. But then, it is like that about everywhere we go. Pastor Treadway and his folks in Abingdon, Virginia, Pastor Fields at Bethany in Thomasville, North Carolina, I could just go on and on forever. Everywhere we go the pastor and his family and his church folks become like a second family to us. I wished everybody in the world knew the kind of preachers and churches we knew. If they did, no one would ever talk bad about Christians.

As I mulled those thoughts over, I snapped back to attention in time to hear dad telling "The Warner Brats" (One of his pet names for us. We don't mind; we know he's kidding.) to load up in the vehicle. Within just a few minutes we were back at the hotel engaging in our normal bedtime preparatory routine. We have had enough years of practice that we are all pretty good at it. The last night of a meeting was always the most difficult, though, because we had to get ready to leave the next day, which meant pre-packing as much stuff as we could the night before. That done, we settled in for another night of sleep for our parents, and another night of adventure for us.

When it came it was such a shock that all three of us screamed. There was a small gash in the side of the plane, and there was smoke filling the cabin. The ebony black sky was laced with the vivid yet dangerous colors of anti-aircraft fire that clearly had a good bead on us. We jumped up just in time to be thrown backward, all the way to the back of the plane, as the Conductor pulled it up hard into a climb that I knew was too drastic for it to make. We landed hard, but had enough presence of mind to hold on tight and start praying our hearts out. We climbed for what seemed like several minutes, and I realized that I was having trouble breathing. I looked at Carrie and Aly and could tell that they were, too. Aly looked sleepy, and I knew that the thin air was knocking her out, she closed her eyes, and I didn't know what to do. Carrie was next, and I could feel myself passing out too...

A few minutes later I came to and realized that I had a mask over my face. To my left I could see that Carrie and Aly did too, and they seemed wide awake now. We looked up into the face of the Conductor, and he seemed relieved that we were ok.

"You scared me, Night Heroes! But I suppose we are even since I scared you pretty badly, too. We almost didn't make it back there."

Groggily I struggled to my feet. "What happened?" I said as I rubbed the back of my head. There was a big bump back there; it was going to make a very nasty knot.

"Apparently our coming and our route was expected on this night. We have had to climb very high to get over top of the anti-aircraft guns," the Conductor said with a grimace.

Now on her feet beside me, Carrie looked trustingly up at him and said, "You did good." Imagine that! With her life on the line my twerp sister was still being an encouragement to others! She is like that most often, which I almost hate to admit since I sometimes forget to be like that.

"Thank you, young lady," he said. And then he dropped a bomb on us. Not a real one, but the impact would not have been any greater if it was.

"I am afraid, though, that we have a problem. We cannot come down to normal altitudes to have you jump. If we attempt to do so, there is no doubt whatsoever that we will be shot down."

Aly gasped and then covered her mouth with her hand. Then she moved her hand to say, "But we have to jump again! Little Miriam is out there waiting for us; we can't let her down! We have told her that we are Christians, and that she can trust us and the Jesus that we serve. We have to jump one more time; we have to!"

She actually stomped her foot a little as she said that, and then she seemed embarrassed that she had done so.

The Conductor just smiled a loving smile. Then he put a hand on top of her head and said, "Young lady, I didn't say you couldn't jump. I said we couldn't go down to normal altitudes to have you jump."

Suddenly I felt myself get very woozy as the meaning of his words sunk in. I dropped down to one knee and felt like I was going to be sick. I almost was, but I made myself not be. I would never hear the end of it if I puked my guts out and my sisters didn't.

The Conductor knelt down beside me, looked me directly in the eyes, and said, "Kyle, I know that you are afraid, and I want to tell you something. It is OK to be afraid. I myself am very often afraid."

Something at that moment made me look very deeply into his eyes. My own eyes grew wide, probably wider than ever in my life. I could see, I knew, it was very clear to me now what he was. If a creature like him could be afraid, then it really was OK. It must have only been a few seconds that I stared into his eyes, but I tell you that it felt like an eternity.

Finally, I came back to myself, and his eyes seemed to be the normal, friendly eyes of our Conductor. I was still scared, but I felt better, much better.

I got up and tried my best to listen, since the Conductor was now all business, telling us what we needed to do to make a high altitude jump. This would not be like before. There would be no static line to open our chutes for us as soon as we jumped. We would be jumping from 8,000 feet this time, nearly a mile and a half high. We would free fall for around twenty seconds and would have to pull our own ripcords at 5,500 feet. We all checked our watches, all of them digital, and we set them on stopwatch.

We stepped near the opening in the side of the plane, and then we knelt to pray. Pray? Oh, boy, did I pray. I am pretty sure I have never prayed like that in my life, ever. My sisters and I, a bunch of untrained kids, were about to jump out of a perfectly good airplane. Not a few hundred feet off of the ground like before, but from a mile and a half high. I prayed for myself. I prayed for Carrie, and as I looked over at her I knew that she was nervous. I also knew that she has the determination and tenacity of a Pit Bull, and that she would kick her fear in the mouth in order to do right. I looked over at Aly and almost, almost decided not to bother praying for her. She was grinning from ear to ear, bouncing like a Chihuahua on Crack. She was actually looking forward to this! Nonetheless, I prayed for her anyway. My sisters mean everything to me. Mom and Dad often tell us that we better love each other, because one day they will be gone and we will be all we have left.

Before I wanted it to be, it was time to jump. I know that the best of my words can never quite describe what it was like, but I'll try. The Conductor had told us that the best thing we could do is take a few steps back from the opening, and when he said "Go" just run out of the door. That would help us not to look down and chicken out. Why, oh why do words like "Go" have to come so quickly?

We ran. We ran like rabbits, and we dove out of the plane into the darkness.

Chapter Twenty-One

Panic. Raw fear. Falling, falling, falling. I forgot to look at my watch! More panic as I realized it may already be too late, and yanked my watch up in front of my face. What?!? It had only been four seconds! Off to my right Carrie was falling and was maybe twenty feet below me. To my left Aly was falling, smooth as silk, in perfect position. Look at the watch. Only seven seconds! More falling. Suddenly I found myself turning over! Not good! Struggle, struggle, reach for something to grab, there is nothing there, grab air, pull, flip back over. Check the watch. Fourteen seconds! I forgot something. What did I forget? My lungs are screaming at me. That's it! Breathing! I forgot to breathe! Take a huge gulp of air. Check the watch. Twenty-one seconds! Pull the cord! Cord? What cord? I was supposed to have the cord in my hand, ready to pull! To my right I heard the "Pop" as Carrie's chute opened. To my left I heard a "Pop" and a "Whoooooooooooooo!" as Aly's chute popped open and she let out a cheer. In the twinkling of an eye I shot past them, still racing toward the ground. The cord! Where was that stinking cord! I flailed and reached and grasped nothingness all around, and suddenly I felt it. When I did, I yanked it, probably harder than anyone has ever yanked a ripcord in the entire history of skydiving!

"Pop!" my chute came open, and my descent was slowed like someone had slammed on the brakes. I looked up at the parachute over my head, smiled in relief...and passed out.

Whap! Whap! Whap! Whap! It was on the fourth "whap" that I recognized the sound, and the feeling that came with it. Someone was slapping me in the face! My eyes snapped open, and I looked up into the terrified eyes of my two sisters. When I opened my eyes, I saw waves of relief wash over their faces. That only lasted for a second for Carrie, who quickly turned back "normal."

"I told you I should have been the one to slap him," she said to Aly. "I could have gotten him awake in two hits or less."

"Pipe down, Sis," I said through gasps, my chest still heaving up and down and my heart still racing a mile a minute while I lay flat on my back. "We have to get up."

"Uh, Big Bro," Aly said gently, "WE don't have to get up. YOU have to get up."

"Uhhhh," I groaned. "I am never, ever doing that again."

Finally I managed to struggle to my feet, and with legs as shaky as a newborn deer, started hauling my gear into the trees, with Little Sis and Littler Sis close behind me.

"Radical! Amazing! Best... night... ever!" I could hear Aly saying to herself, the trees, the bunnies, whoever or whatever was near enough to hear.

"Quite, Sis," Carrie said with a smile in her voice. "Yeah, it was great, but we still have to avoid being captured long enough to rescue Miriam. That means that you need to be quiet."

Forty-five minutes later we reached the spot in the trees where Miriam would be waiting for us. The sun was just coming up, its rays filtering through the towering trees of the forests of northern Germany. Miriam, bless her little heart, was still lying under the tree fast asleep as the rays of the morning gently touched her cheeks.

"Funny, isn't it?"

I looked over at Carrie and said, "What do you mean?"

"This is the woman that will raise the son that helps to save Israel in one of her darkest hours. But right now she's just a precious little

129

girl. It's just amazing that God knows each of us and what we are going to do with our lives."

"Now that you put it that way," I said, "it is kind of amazing. We have to get her up, though, every second is critical."

And so we did. Ten minutes later we were walking, very slowly, very carefully. We went from tree to tree. We crawled on our bellies through gullies. We had to get as close to the town as we could without being noticed. We covered the mile or so to the edge of the town in a little over three hours.

Then we began the work of scanning, looking, evaluating, seeing what we were up against and what we would have to do. The seagulls over the harbor sang their shrill song, while the salt air wafted over us. The town was medium sized. All the buildings were made of wood, wood that had been salt treated by nature from years of exposure to sea breezes. The boards were all a dull gray, except for the boards on the sidewalks, which seemed to have a relatively recent coat of green paint. We could not understand the signs, but most of the buildings seemed to explain themselves. The one with men going into it with shaggy hair and coming out a bit later with short hair was obviously the barber shop. Off to the left and stretching away in an arc down the coastline were other non-descript buildings, and after perhaps a tenth of a mile or so we saw the dock

130

with a passenger ship securely fastened to it. The gang plank was down onto the dock itself, and various workers were loading supplies onto it. This was it, our goal was in sight! If we could get Miriam onto that ship, she would be safe and our task would be done.

But then we saw them, the line of gray/green army trucks with the swastikas on the side. Six of them. They drove into the middle of town, way too fast, and came to a screeching halt. At least twelve German soldiers came piling out of each one, all of them carrying wicked-looking machine guns. They began to bark orders, and everyone in their path instantly obeyed them, whether that meant they were to get out of the way or to move a vehicle or to carry a pack for them. At least two dozen of those soldiers ran to the dock. Two of them took up positions by the gang plank, guns pointed outward. The rest stormed aboard the ship, and we could hear screaming and shouting as they rummaged through every room, slapping people around, barking orders, and generally being the bullies that they were famous for being.

I looked over at Carrie and Aly, and they looked over at little Miriam. When they did, she shook her head and spoke softly. "So close, we came so close..."

"Hey," I whispered half out loud to her, "look at me. This isn't over."

"Yes, it is," she said sadly and with a hint of fear in her voice. "They clearly knew we were headed here and what we had in mind. When they cannot find me aboard the ship, they will leave the guards in place, and then they will search the town. When they cannot find me in the town, they will come into the trees. And I can assure you that there are already soldiers coming this way through the trees from behind us. With Hitler, every Jewish escapee is an intensely personal matter. We are trapped. They are behind us, before us, and around us. There is no escape."

"Miriam," Aly said with a smile, "you aren't the first Israelite to be in such a predicament. In fact, your entire nation was in just such a fix nearly 4,000 years ago. I know you must have read about it in the book of Exodus. They were by the sea then just like we are now, only then it was the Red Sea instead of the Baltic Sea. Pharaoh's army was behind and all around them, using all of their might to take them back into captivity. But your Jehovah, our Jesus, stepped in and parted the sea, and they escaped. Then He collapsed the sea back in on the armies that were chasing them, and they were never bothered by them again. Do you remember that? Do you believe it?"

"Yes, I do remember it," she said, "and yes, I do believe it. I just do not know if it is possible again. Nor, by the way, am I convinced that my Jehovah is actually your Jesus!"

And then it hit me. "Miriam," I said, "will you promise me something? If our God does deliver you, whether it be by parting the sea, or by some much more mundane 'miracle,' will you promise to at least consider the issue? Will you promise to read the Bible and study up on Jesus? I ask this for a reason. I believe that Jesus is able to show us a way of escape for you. And I also believe that He hears me when I pray. We are going to pray, Miriam, my sisters and I are going to pray right now to Jesus. He has brought us this far with you, and I believe that if we pray, He will show us how to get you past those soldiers, onto that boat, and to safety. If He does, will you promise to do what I asked? Will you at least consider Jesus?"

Without so much as a moment's hesitation she said, "I promise. And I do so simply because I know that if I get safely on that boat, it will be a miracle, and therefore, God must be involved. Yes, pray. If your Jesus answers, I will consider Him."

And so we prayed right there a few feet inside the tree line, not loud enough to be heard by anyone in the town, only in voices barely above a whisper. In other words, we prayed and knew that Miriam heard every word, and that our Jesus heard us as well as if we had been shouting at the top of our lungs. We prayed for wisdom; we prayed for safety. We prayed that the Lord would do for one little descendant of Abraham what He did for all of them 4,000 years ago. Finally, our words were done, and we, as we do often in prayer, just lay there before the Lord, feeling His presence, basking in it like laying in the sunshine on a beautiful spring day.

And then I heard it. Laughter. Carrie was beside me, laughing softly. We all looked over at her, wondering. I knew that she would never be disrespectful during prayer, and that left only one option in my mind. I grinned at her and asked, "Is this going to be as interesting as I think it is?"

"Oh, yeah," she replied. "I think the word 'interesting' would certainly be applicable. I think the Lord has just given me an idea. A crazy, no, scratch that, an *insane* idea. So insane that I know for a fact I didn't think it up myself."

"Details, Sis, details!" Aly said.

"Well," she said, "the Nazis are looking for a little girl. I think we ought to give her to them."

"What?!?" we all said in stunned disbelief.

"Sis, have you lost your mind?" I asked. "We've gone through our own private Tribulation Period to rescue Miriam, and your plan is to hand her over to them? Seriously?"

"I didn't say that," Carrie answered while looking over at Miriam with a reassuring smile. Miriam, for her part, seemed not to know what to make of any of this. "I said that we ought to give the Nazis a little girl. I doubt seriously if they have any photos of Miriam, it's not like concentration camps use mug shots. All they are likely to have is a general description of her. If we gave them someone the same general size and shape, wearing her clothes from the concentration camp, they would not know they had been duped until it is too late. I can do this, Bro, I can use myself as bait to get Miriam on that boat."

"Absolutely not!" I practically shouted. "I am not sacrificing you for anyone else. No offense, Miriam," I said as I looked over at her.

"None taken," she replied. "I happen to agree with you. No one should have to die for me."

"For starters, Miriam," Carrie said with a smile, "Someone already did die for you. His name is Jesus, and when He went to Calvary, it was for you. You promised us you would look into it once God makes a way for you to get on that boat, so I recommend that you do so. You can start in your Old Testament, Isaiah 53. That is a prophetic description of the crucifixion written hundreds of years before it happened. But secondly, I don't actually plan to die. What I plan to do is draw them away so that you can get on that boat. Give us a minute, please, I need to talk to Aly and Kyle alone."

With that we walked a ways back into the trees, and Carrie told us what she had in mind. I could not help but let out a low whistle as I shook my head in amazement. "That is crazy, Sis, rabid bat kind of crazy. But it might just be crazy enough to work. I still don't like it though, not at all. What if it doesn't work?

"Look," she said firmly, "it has to. The Conductor has told us the rules. Once we go to sleep after a certain time of day, we instantly wake up in our own time, as long as we are not being held captive in this time. The timing will need to be perfect, though. If we can do everything just right, it will give Miriam the time she needs to slip onto the boat undetected and will still get us back safely. Well, at least sort of safely."

We walked back over to Miriam, brought her back into the trees with us well out of sight, and then I went a way back into the trees to let the girls switch clothes in private. They made the switch, and then called everyone together. We explained to Miriam what we intended to do, at least the parts that we could tell her, and then we went to work.

Chapter Twenty-Two

Part one of our plan required a lot of boldness, or what my dad would call "hiding in plain sight." In the midst of all of the soldiers bustling about, I casually strolled into town, acting as if I belonged. I kept reminding myself that no one was looking for one boy, everyone was looking for a boy and three girls. Oftentimes you can simply act like you should be doing what you are doing, and no one will even question it. I went into what I knew was a general store/clothing store type of business. I could tell this because of the lovely plate glass window displaying the store's wares. It was the only plate glass window in town, and I trusted that this would work to our advantage. This first part of the plan we had chosen to call "Little David Uses a Second Stone." Mulling about the store, I located all of the items I would need. Then I looked at my stopwatch and saw that in twenty-seven seconds the first diversion would come. I mulled about some more, staying close to the items I would need, and silently counting down from twenty-seven.

Right on cue, Aly, from her hiding place not too far off in the trees, let loose with her slingshot. Of all three of us kids, I must tell you that Aly is by far the best with a slingshot. Please don't ever give her a reason to fire a rock at you, because I promise, she is not going to miss.

Crack! Went the pane glass window. Aly had zinged her carefully chosen rock right over the head of two soldiers standing outside and had hit the glass dead center. A nasty crack like a spider web was now spreading out across it. The owner of the store shouted in anger and rushed outside to confront the soldiers that he was certain had broken the glass. And why not? They were making a mess all over the rest of the town; they were the obvious ones to blame.

I did not waste a second. While he was outside screaming at them, with them screaming right back and obviously threatening him, I snatched up two hats, two pairs of boys pants, two boys shirts, and stuffed them under my shirt. Then I tossed all of the German money in my pocket onto the counter to pay for the clothes and the broken glass and ran out the back way. I now looked like a fat kid waddling down the shoreline toward the east. I went about a half a mile, then turned right and headed back for the trees. Once I got into the trees it was a half mile back to the rendezvous spot. I turned away while Miriam and Aly got dressed like boys, and then when they were done I turned back to them and had them put the hats on, stuffing their long hair inside them. To anyone who was not looking closely, they would be able to pass for boys. And it was up to Carrie to make sure that no one was looking closely.

A few minutes later it was time to sink or swim, and frighteningly enough, this was not metaphorical for Carrie.

Miriam and Aly and I made our way just inside the tree line toward the west until we were at the nearest point to the ship. Then we crouched down, let out a low whistle, and Carrie went to work.

Please don't ever let me forget how brave my sister is. For all of the grief I give her (what are brothers for?) I really do admire her. Without any hesitation at all, she got up and began walking, right out in the open toward the shore line, angling off to the east away from the ship. We all knew it was just a matter of time before she was spotted. Sure enough, one of those evil German soldiers spotted her, and shouted something in German that could not possibly be good. He started toward her, and she bolted like a scared rabbit. We were really counting on them chasing her rather than shooting at her. If they started shooting, I had already made up my mind to go ballistic on all of them, even if I got killed myself!

It wasn't necessary. Just as we had hoped, when she bolted and ran the soldiers immediately gave chase. Let me tell you, my sister is fast, especially when she is scared. She was practically flying across the sand, and I kid you not, every single German soldier gave chase.

Immediately we were up and out of hiding. We half strolled half ran down to the ship, and no one gave us "three boys" any notice at all. We rushed up the gang plank, and as planned, all three of us piled into a life boat and pulled the cover back over it and us good and snug. Our breaths were still coming in heaves, but we knew we had to calm down. We had to calm down enough to pray, Carrie was still very much in danger. We also had to calm down enough to get Miriam to sleep, so that we could go to sleep and get home without her seeing us vanish before her eyes.

Chapter Twenty-Three

Hey, this is Carrie, I'll take it from here, since Kyle and Aly were not able to see what was happening with me. As soon as the soldiers gave chase, I ran, putting Operation Jonah into play. I wanted to get a good quarter mile or so away from the ship in order to give Kyle and Aly and Miriam time to get on board and under cover. Looking back over my shoulder I could see the soldiers gaining on me. I knew it was about time to go for a swim. I turned left on a dime and bolted into the water. Friends, my dad has taught all of us to swim like fishes, and I did so now. The concentration camp dress I was wearing was quickly water soaked and heavy, but I knew the soldiers splashing in after me would be at a similar disadvantage with their heavy uniforms and boots. I swam, oh did I swim, straight out to sea! I knew the soldiers had to think I was either insane or suicidal or both. Where was this crazy little girl going to go? Did she think she could swim across the Baltic Sea to safety?

I swam. I swam hard. Looking back over my shoulder, I could see three soldiers swimming after me, with the rest on shore cheering them on. They knew they could catch me, they were trained soldiers and I was just a scared little girl from a concentration camp.

Only I'm not. I am a Night Hero, and I had no intention of being taken to Ravensbruck or anywhere else these goons wanted to take me.

I had gotten probably a hundred yards offshore, when suddenly I turned to face my aquatic pursuers. I smiled at them, then I breathed in and out really hard and fast seven or eight times and sank down beneath the dark waves, letting them swallow me in their cold, death like grip.

Chapter Twenty-Four

Hey, this is Kyle, I'll pick the story back up now. The first sound I heard was the oh, so comforting sound of the air conditioner droning steadily at the Fayetteville Inn and Suites. I looked over and checked, and Aly, but only Aly, was laying in the girl's bed. I gasped, immediately in full panic mode. Then I heard a familiar voice coming from the corner, shushing me quietly. I looked over, and thank God, Carrie was sitting there.

"I had to real quietly get out of those wet clothes, get rid of them, and get into some dry ones," she said.

"Then it worked? It really worked?"

"Like clockwork. Seven or eight hard breaths and I hyperventilate and pass out, just like always. It has always been an accident before; it's nice to know that I can do it intentionally if I need to. Although," she added, "with the massive headache it has given me, I sure hope I never have to do it again."

When Carrie passed out asleep in the water, it immediately brought her back to our time. The soldiers would never know what happened; they would simply think that little Miriam had drowned. The ship would be able to sail all the way to Sweden with her on it without any risk of anyone even looking for her; she was safe.

"Wow! That was amazing!" Aly said in a whisper, just coming out of her groggy sleep. "Especially what happened in the boat!"

I said, "I agree, Littlest Sis, that was absolutely the best part."

"What? What do you mean 'what happened in the boat?' I thought all of the excitement was happening out there in the water where I was drowning/disappearing. What happened?"

I smiled a great big smile as I began to tell Carrie that little Miriam had been rescued in more ways than one, and that we would most definitely see her again one day.

Coming Soon
In 2014

The Night Heroes Book Three
Broken Brotherhood

Two or three more seconds and he would pull the trigger and end his brother's life. Suddenly there was a flash of movement from off to the right. It was Kyle!

Kyle came diving in at full speed, smashing right into his side. The gun went off, and both Kyle and he went tumbling over the edge of the hill—a fighting, grasping, undistinguishable mass of fists and feet…

Meet the Author

Dr. Wagner is the founder and pastor of Cornerstone Baptist Church of Mooresboro, North Carolina. He was saved in 1979 and began preaching regularly as a twelve-year-old boy in 1982.

He earned an Associate's Degree in Communications Technology from Cleveland Community College in 1989. He earned his Bachelor's Degree in Pastoral Studies with highest honors in 1997 and then his Master's and Doctorate with highest honors from Carolina Bible College in 2001 and 2003. He founded Cornerstone Baptist Church in 1997. He has been teaching at the Carolina Bible College since 2000 and has been a professor since 2003.

He has been writing books since 2009, with Cry from the Coal Mine being his first fiction book.

Along with pastoring, Dr. Wagner preaches in many revivals, camp meetings, and family conferences each year.

He married Dana in 1994. They have three Children: Caleb, Karis, and Aléthia.

Other Books in the Night Heroes Series

Cry From the Coal Mine

Broken Brotherhood
(coming in 2014)